12 HOURS OF HALLOWEEN

EDWARD TRIMNELL

"The youths were consumed by the fire, so that no one was to hear their wedding songs."

Psalms 78:63

PROLOGUE

A funny thing about flashbacks: they come unbidden, and at the most unexpected times.

One moment I was standing in Walmart, and the next moment I was not: I was a twelve-year-old boy again, crouching beside the outer wall of a darkened house in a long-ago suburb, hoping that the shrubbery to my right and my left had adequately concealed my presence. A malevolent creature was intent on taking my head. He—or it—had an entire sack full of them.

That particular flashback is always especially vivid. When it overtakes me, I can feel not only the pervasive, all-consuming fear of those eternal minutes, but also the little details of my surroundings: the cold, damp ground beneath me, the scratchy feel of the barren shrubbery of late October.

This is one reason why I still believe that it really did happen—even after all these years. A delusion wouldn't include so many little details.

AND THEN, in the next second, the flashback is gone: I'm no longer that crouching, quivering twelve-year-old boy. I'm a grown man in my mid-forties—solidly into middle age by any yardstick. I'm no longer crouching in the dark: I'm standing yet again in the fluorescent glare of the Walmart near my home in Cincinnati, shopping for a calculator.

Although I knew that I would come back (I always do!), it's good to be back, nonetheless.

The calculator that I'm looking for is not just any calculator; it's a TI-89 graphing calculator, one of the models that Texas Instruments designed especially for engineers. Don't ask me how to use the thing, or about its features. I would have no idea. The calculator is for my daughter, Lisa. Lisa turns twenty on the third of November, during the week after Halloween.

Lisa is a student at the University of Cincinnati, and an engineering major. She's a lot smarter than her dad, I don't mind saying— even though her dad hasn't done badly for himself, all things considered. But Lisa gets her smarts from her mother, who has always been good at math.

Lisa has a younger sister, Hannah. Hannah graduates from high school next year. Hannah takes after her father more, which is to say she's not so good at math. But she's creative and more of a "people person" than her older sister. I look for Hannah to major in business administration or political science. Something like that. We'll see. She has a year to decide.

Last week Hannah and I were talking about the future, and she shared her anxieties with me. It's so competitive out there nowadays —nothing like the days of my youth, when any college degree would enable you to blunder your way into some sort of a professional career. And Hannah has always felt that she lives in Lisa's shadow. Her older sister was always the one with the straight A's—the one with the academic awards. Throughout grade school and high school, hardly a one of Hannah's teachers failed to remember and mention her "gifted" older sibling.

"Maybe I'll end up selling insurance with you, Dad," Hannah said. She said this in jest, but it's not a half-bad idea: My State Farm agency has brought in a good living over the past seventeen years. (I drifted into insurance sales after several false starts in other fields.) "Maybe you will," I said. "Your old man would be glad to have you."

Who knows? Hannah's still in high school, and her preferences might end up channeled in one of any number of directions. But it's something for us both to keep in mind.

I'm walking toward the Walmart's electronics section when I catch a brief glimpse of the head collector in the rear area of the store —through the double doorway marked "Employees Only". He's standing there by a bare cinderblock wall, near one of the warehouse area's fire extinguishers. The fire extinguisher enables me to gage his height: seven or eight feet, just like he's always been.

I pause to rub my eyes, and look again: The head collector is gone, just as I knew would be the case.

It's not uncommon for me to see the head collector at this time of year. I only see him briefly—and never up close. If I saw him up close, well, that might be enough to drive me over the edge. Far away, he's an anxiety that I can live with.

Keep calm, I tell myself: I focus on Hannah and Lisa, and my wife of twenty-two years. I focus on purchasing the calculator for Lisa's birthday.

Halloween is often a difficult time for me, though the flashbacks are only this vivid every third or fourth year.

The atmosphere inside the Walmart isn't helping matters. There are only a few days remaining before October 31st, and the store is filled with every conceivable trapping of Halloween: There are cardboard black cats with arched backs and erect tails. Near a display of trick-or-treat candy, a mechanical life-size plastic witch with green skin and a jutting chin and nose twists back and forth. And everywhere there are jack-o'-lanterns: plastic hollow jack-o'-lanterns for collecting candy, inflatable jack-o'-lanterns to be used as lawn decorations—even some jack-o'-lantern-shaped candles.

My individual traumas aside, I note that Halloween doesn't change much. Well over thirty Halloweens have passed since what I consider to be my "last Halloween" in 1980 (*the Halloween that I'm going to tell you about shortly*); but the basics of that dark holiday don't change much, do they? Halloween is impervious to the Internet, to the vagaries of politics and pop culture. Halloween is dark, eternal, and yes, strangely inviting. *(That was why Leah and Bobby and I decided to indulge in that "last Halloween", even though we were really too old for it by then. We didn't want to let Halloween go—not quite yet.)*

I finally reach the electronics section. It has been my observation that Walmart's "everyday low prices" are at least partly achieved by minimizing the number of sales clerks on the floor at any given time. But I'm in luck: there is a salesperson behind the electronics counter. She's a young woman about Lisa's age, maybe a few years older.

"I'm looking for a TI-89 graphing calculator," I tell her from memory. *(Again, I am absolutely clueless about such things.)*

"Well, sir, we have that model in stock."

It doesn't take long for me to select Lisa's calculator and pay for it. The total comes to $146.78 with tax. Throughout our brief interaction, the sales clerk calls me "mister" and "sir" any number of times, pointedly reminding me of my age. Not that I mind. There is only one woman for me: my wife; so I don't care if the young sales clerk thinks I'm an old guy. And if being called sir is the price of having two wonderful daughters, then may the whole world call me sir.

That done, I collect my purchase inside its white plastic Walmart bag, and head for the main exit. On the way out I pass another sales clerk. She's a bit older and rather on the chubby side.

As I'm about to push one of the glass doors open I hear her say, *"Hey, you're going to lose your head!"*

I whirl around, my heart suddenly beating rapidly. *The head collector*, I think.

But she looks at me innocently.

"You dropped your receipt," she says, pointing to a small strip of paper on the floor. Now I understand: What the clerk had really said was, "You lost your receipt"—or something very similar.

I stoop and pick up the receipt.

"Thank you," I say.

I'm out in the parking lot, glad to be done with Walmart and all those Halloween decorations. I think again about the head collector, and how I caught that brief sight of him in the back of the store. Would he follow me out here?

The skies above me are overcast and grey; but it's a little after 10:00 a.m.—broad daylight. (Another perk of self-employment: You can do your shopping at 10 o'clock on a Tuesday morning, when the rest of the world is otherwise engaged.) The head collector wouldn't follow me out here. That is not his way.

I start my car, a pearl white Toyota Avalon. Yes, it's a middle-aged man's car. Hannah jokingly refers to it as my "Avillac". You get it? A combination of Avalon and Cadillac.

I drive home, thinking mostly good thoughts: My two nearly grown daughters, my wife. Maybe I'll make love to my wife tonight, I think. (I may be a middle-aged man, but I'm a long, long way from being too old for *that*.)

But inevitably, I find myself thinking of the past, too. I think about Bobby and Leah. I think about the head collector, of course.

And I think about Matt Stefano. Yes, I really hate to think about *him*.

1

"You wanna die, Schaeffer? You wanna die right now? Because I can kill you, you know. And there's nothing that anyone can do about it. Would you like that?"

Although Stefano had no doubt intended the question to be purely rhetorical, I shook my head, even as Stefano tightened his grip around my shirt collar, making it more difficult for me to breathe. Nor did I really believe that Matt Stefano would kill me—though there were times when I wondered. But it would not be beyond him to hurt me very, very badly. Matt Stefano, I believed, was either seriously crazy or pathologically evil—and possibly both.

Behind me, I could feel the brick wall of the rear side of St. Patrick's Elementary School. Why had I been stupid enough to wander back here after eating lunch? When you're a twelve-year-old boy who is trying to dodge a bully, there is *always* safety in numbers. You want to be out in the open, where everyone can see everything and everyone.

The rest of the seventh and eighth graders—not to mention two or three *teachers*—were on the other side of the building. But they might as well have been a mile or two away. Back here, beneath the late autumn shade of the pin oak trees that dominated the rear of the school building, it was only Matt Stefano and I.

"Do you wanna die?" he repeated. "*Do* you?"

What did he expect me to say? I might have pointed out, for instance, that this was far from a fair fight. Matt Stefano was not only an eighth grader—but an eighth grader who had been held back at least once. *(And there were persistent rumors that he had been held back* twice *along the way.)* So I was twelve years old, and he was fourteen or fifteen. At that age among boys, two or three years of growth confers a big advantage.

Add to that the fact that Stefano was a naturally big boy. He was by far the tallest of the eighth graders, coming in at just over six feet and perhaps a hundred and eighty pounds or so. He could easily have been an athlete, but it was clear that Matt Stefano much preferred to be a hoodlum. He wore his hair long, even as long hair was now starting to pass out of style, a remnant of the recent sixties and seventies.

In those adolescent years in which the concepts of sex appeal and popularity are nascent, Matt wasn't quite a heartthrob. Not quite. That honor was reserved for the more clean-cut, mainstream boys who excelled at basketball and baseball. But Stefano definitely had a following among both the seventh and eighth grade girls.

While I waited for Matt Stefano to do his worst, I had a random thought: Why had my parents sent me to St. Patrick's Elementary School in the first place—instead of the nearby public school, Youngman Elementary?

Certainly they had wanted me to get a Catholic education. At St. Patrick's we wore the typical Catholic school uniforms: white shirts and dark slacks for the boys, plaid skirts and white blouses for the girls. We attended mass once a week, and one of our regular courses was indeed called Religion—a mixture of church history, Bible study, and current events from a Catholic perspective. My parents were both devoted Roman Catholics, so that was important to them.

But maybe, I thought, they also wanted to spare me the indignity of being held against a wall by a school bully like Matt Stefano. What was he even doing at St. Patrick's, I wondered? Who had signed the papers that had allowed him in here?

This town, Withamsville, was not even a town, properly speaking, but a "census-designated place" not far from the Cincinnati city limits. Withamsville was a mixed income community where the old money neighborhoods of the city bled into a semirural zone of body shops, trailer parks, and pony kegs. Withamsville was neither city nor farmland, but a no-man's land where newly built suburbs mingled with postwar tract homes, and still older, decaying neighborhoods inhabited by the sons of Appalachian migrants, and white-flight refugees who had fled the poorer sections of the city following the race riots of the 1960s. It was a world that was alternately refined and rough, where upper middle class kids like me often fell prey to working class bullies like Matt Stefano.

That was about the time when we both heard the rock crash against the wall, not so very far from Matt's left ear. The sound immediately captured both our attention, and Matt temporarily relaxed his grip on me. But he didn't let go.

Matt turned around, and there was Bobby Nagel. He wasn't on top of us, but he was within sprinting distance. *The cavalry*, I thought, or something like that.

"What are you doin', Nagel?" Stefano growled. "Did you throw that rock at me?"

"Naw, I just threw the rock," Bobby said evenly. "If I'd have wanted to hit you, I'd have hit you."

I was more than a little amazed—and more than a little admiring—of the way Bobby stood there, staring down Matt Stefano. Bobby was only an inch taller than me, but he was a scrapper with a fair share of fisticuffs on his adolescent resume. Like Matt Stefano, Bobby came from what was then called "a broken home". Although Bobby and I were friends, I had met his father perhaps once or twice; and Bobby claimed to see the man only rarely.

"Come on, Matt," Bobby said. "Let him go. He ain't bothering you."

Matt now held me by the collar with one hand. He punctuated his next question by pointing his finger at Bobby.

"Or *what*, Nagel? Are you going to *make* me?"

Bobby paused to contemplate this. He was a lot tougher than I was; but he was no match for Matt Stefano.

"A teacher's headed this way, you know," Bobby said, dodging the direct challenge.

"Bullshit! You're *bluffing!*"

"But what if I'm not, Matt? How many more demerits for you before you get suspended, huh? How many before they throw your ass out of here, and you're off to Youngman Elementary with the other *criminals?*"

"You son of a bitch!" Matt yelled. "I'll *kill* you!"

The subtext of Bobby's insult had not gone unnoticed. When he called Matt a criminal, he did not mean the term in its generic sense. Everyone at school knew that Matt Stefano's father, Tony Stefano, had recently been arrested and charged with burglary in Cincinnati. The elder Stefano was presently doing time at Lebanon Correctional Institute, about fifty miles north of Cincinnati. Bobby's reference, however oblique it may have been, had touched a raw nerve.

I was sure that Matt was going to charge Bobby, or perhaps take out this new wave of anger on me. Then Mr. Malinowski came into view. Bobby had not been bluffing about the teacher, after all.

I hadn't seen Mr. Malinowski approach. That wasn't really surprising, though, given that Matt Stefano had me pressed up against the side of the building.

"What's going on here?" Mr. Malinowski asked. That much was fairly obvious, wasn't it?

"Nothin'!" Matt said, instantly releasing me. Though Matt Stefano was easily the toughest and most feared kid at St. Patrick's, he wouldn't directly challenge a teacher. That simply wasn't done. A hoodlum like Stefano might get by with thinly veiled sarcasm and the occasional lie; but had he physically confronted a teacher, he would have been out of the school and off to Youngman—or maybe even reform school. Just as Bobby had said.

"It didn't look like 'nothin'" to me," Mr. Malinowski said. He was well into his fifties, but Mr. Malinowski was a big man. Moreover, I could tell that he didn't like Matt Stefano. None of the teachers did, really; but Mr. Malinowski's tone suggested a degree of antipathy that extended beyond an educator's professional exasperation with an incurable problem student. Reflecting on this moment years later, I would sometimes wonder if there had been a Matt Stefano in Mr. Malinowski's childhood. That would have explained a lot.

Mr. Malinowski, ignoring Bobby for the most part, walked closer to Matt Stefano and me. Matt now took a deliberate step away from me, as if to demonstrate his innocence.

Without warning, Mr. Malinowski grabbed Matt by his shirt collar, and shoved him up against the building, much as Matt had been doing to me a minute ago.

"Picking on other kids again?" Mr. Malinowski asked, bringing his face to within inches of Stefano's. "Maybe you ought to try picking on someone your own size—someone who can fight back."

I know what you're probably thinking about now: There is so much about this entire exchange that would be impossible nowadays, or would result in multiple lawsuits.

But keep in mind: this was the early 1980s. Nearly two decades before Columbine, schools were much less vigilant about bullying. Unless one of the victims really made an issue of a bullying problem, the schools tended to make students work out these problems among themselves.

And as for a teacher laying hands on a child in a threatening manner: Corporal punishment was still practiced in many schools in 1980, and no one thought anything of parents spanking their own children. Not like nowadays, when spanking has become a matter for media worrywarts and United Nations human rights lawyers.

I was half-expecting Mr. Malinowski to throw a punch at Matt Stefano, but instead he let the boy go and shoved him away. Even in the early 1980s, a punch from a teacher would have constituted an "incident". I also wondered, briefly, if Matt would have retaliated at that point, and what the outcome might have been. At six-foot-three and maybe two hundred and forty pounds, Mr. Malinowski was somewhat the larger of the two. But Matt was younger, probably faster, and almost certainly meaner.

"Don't let me catch you doing that again, Stefano," Mr. Malinowski said. "And to help you remember, I'm going to write up three demerits for you. They should add nicely to your total."

By this time I had moved away from Matt Stefano and Mr. Malinowski. I was standing next to Bobby. Mr. Malinowski turned to Bobby and me. "Why don't you two boys join the rest of the students in the front area of the school grounds," he said. "Lunchtime is almost over."

This was a command, not a request, though both Bobby and I were more than happy to comply. I shuffled away, Bobby at my side, while Mr. Malinowski continued his lecture at Matt Stefano. The teacher's intervention had been a mixed blessing: On one hand, I had been saved from immediate peril. On the other hand, though, I had (however indirectly and without fault) subjected Matt to three demerits and humiliating treatment at the hands of an adult authority figure. Matt would be looking for a payback.

"Why does that guy have it out for you so much?" Bobby asked.

I shrugged. "Doesn't he have it out for everybody, when you think about it?"

"I guess," Bobby said. The truth, though, was that Bobby had never directly incurred Matt Stefano's wrath. Matt might have been able to whip Bobby easily, if it came to that; but Matt's favorite targets were the boys who lived in the newly built neighborhoods in Withamsville, the sons of attorneys, engineers, and corporate middle managers. It was a form of classism in reverse, though back then I wouldn't have expressed the situation in those terms.

We made it to the front area of the school grounds just as the other teachers were summoning the seventh and eighth grade kids back into the building for the afternoon's classes. It was one of those golden October days that hover just on the edge of summertime warmth. (That brief period from mid-September through late October is the only truly beautiful season in Ohio.) There was a small breeze, and the big trees that ringed the school grounds were an explosion of red, bronze, and burnt yellow. Neither of us was anxious to go back inside, where we would sweat inside the basement classrooms.

"I guess we should enjoy our recesses while we still can," Bobby said, as if reading my mind. At St. Patrick's all students from grades one through eight were given twenty minutes of outdoor time in the morning, followed by approximately half an hour after lunch. "There's no recess in high school. Not at Bishop Stallings. Not at Youngman, either."

Although Bobby was referring to the weather, his mention of the two high schools raised an uncomfortable truth: After next year, we would be parting ways, as I headed off to Bishop Stallings High School, and Bobby headed off to Youngman High School, the high school equivalent of Youngman Elementary.

Bobby—like many of the lower income kids at St. Patrick's—received defrayed tuition from a parish grant. But Bishop Stallings was a consolidated Cincinnati archdiocese high school, and it cost serious money to attend. While the tuition was not an insurmountable burden for my parents, it was hopelessly beyond the reach of Bobby Nagel's mother. And as for his father contributing—well, that notion was so unlikely that it was never even broached. According to my mother, Joyce Nagel was lucky to collect two or three child support payments per year from Bobby's errant father.

"You might wonder why I did that," Bobby said, clapping me on the shoulder. "I mean—sticking up for you like that."

"Of course I know what you mean," I said. "Thanks."

"Well, I didn't do it for you," Bobby said. "I did it for me. I figure that Matt Stefano and I are bound to mix it up sooner or later."

"Bobby. You can't whip Matt Stefano."

"Exactly." Bobby clapped me on the shoulder again. "I figure I'll show him that I'm not afraid of him now, while we're both here at St. Patrick's. Then when we're at Youngman together, he'll leave me alone."

That logic didn't make sense to me. Matt Stefano wasn't the type to forget a grudge. On the contrary, he would spend the next two years calculating the interest on his vendetta against Bobby.

Moreover, while Matt's "gang" at St. Patrick's was limited to a handful of hoodlumish eighth grade boys, at Youngman he would be among his own element. By the time Bobby faced him there, Matt would be part of a regular gang of like-minded delinquents; and boys of that ilk had no qualms about fighting with unequal numbers.

It occurred to me that this might be Bobby's way of making me feel less awkward than I already did about him functioning as my unofficial bodyguard.

I merely nodded. "Well, thanks anyway. I was in a jam back there."

We were drawing near to the mass of other students now, who were filing into the seventh and eighth grade classrooms of St. Patrick's in two single-file rows. The lower grades were taught in a separate building—a much older red brick structure that was built around the turn of the (twentieth) century. The junior high classrooms were housed beneath the church. That building had been built in the mid-1960s, so it was still fairly newish in 1980.

As was now my habit, I began to look for Leah. I had known Leah most of my life, and I had seen her on a daily basis since kindergarten, more or less. But that had all changed lately: each time I saw her it was now a special event. This was a season in my life in which I would often lay awake at night, wondering if Leah Carter might ever feel the same way.

I could not find Leah among the two queues of students. She must already be inside. Thankfully, no Matt Stefano, either. *(The latter was likely still being detained by Mr. Malinowski.)* I took my place in line, behind Stephanie Santangelo and Julie Brinson. I tried not to stare at their legs, which (as lots of campy male fantasy literature has made much of in the intervening years) were visible in their Catholic school girls' skirts. Both sets of legs still bore the deep brown of the recent summer's tan.

How long had it been since girls' legs had been of any interest to me at all? Less than a year, I would say—and now I was all but obsessed with them. Not only girls' legs, mind you, but their hair, their voices, and the degree to which they were "developed".

Only a year or so ago, my sole concerns had been summer little league, comic books, and playing video games like pong and stunt cycle. (A few Christmases ago, my parents had presented me with a *Telegames* console from Sears. Crude by today's standards, it was a forerunner of the Atari video game consoles that would take the country by storm within a few years.) But now I noticed seemingly every girl I came into contact with, and I was constantly trying to gauge their reaction to *me*.

I followed the flow of people inside. We passed through the main foyer of the building, past the staircase that led up to the church proper. Looking upward, I caught a waft of incense, and a glimpse of the statue of the Blessed Virgin, her arms outstretched, a serpent crushed beneath her sandaled feet.

We students went downstairs instead, toward the classrooms. I was passing through the downstairs doorway, still sneaking glances at Stephanie and Julie when I felt a much larger presence brush past me, deliberately knocking me into the doorframe.

Matt Stefano surged past me without doing further damage for now, elbowing his way through the crowd. But he did take the time to look back and glare at me; and his message was clear: It wasn't over between us; no—it wasn't over by a long shot.

2

I put Matt Stefano and my troubles with him out of my mind as I prepared for my afternoon classes. Yes—I was still afraid of him; but now I was also thinking about Leah, whom I would see in the first of my afternoon classes.

I walked down the hall toward Mr. Snyder's classroom. The surrounding walls were decorated for Halloween: cardboard ghosts, jack-o'-lanterns, and haunted houses—all the usual clichés.

Was twelve years old too old for Halloween? I wondered. My father certainly seemed to think so. When I announced, several weeks ago, that Leah and Bobby and I were planning one last trick-or-treat, he gave me that gentle, fatherly disapproving look of his and shook his head. My father was a member of a very different generation, and he had some equally different ideas about the proper lines between childhood and adulthood. I was certain that I hadn't heard the last from him on the issue.

And I was ambivalent myself about this year's trick-or-treat being a threesome of Bobby, Leah, and I, even though it had always been so, ever since we were little kids. I would have much preferred it be just Leah and I.

As I walked into Mr. Snyder's classroom, the teacher was jotting some notes on the chalkboard. This was seventh grade religion class. Although we sometimes discussed church history and theology, Mr. Snyder was one of those "free ranging" teachers who liked to incorporate plenty of discussions about current events, too.

And in that fall of 1980, there were plenty of contentious current events to discuss: Since the previous November, fifty-two American embassy personnel had been held hostage in Iran. That provoked the question: Should the U.S. bomb Iran, or try to make a deal? Most of the boys in the class seemed to think that the US should send in the bombers. Mr. Snyder urged a more cautious course.

"Don't forget," Mr. Snyder admonished. "President Carter did attempt to respond with force last spring. Operation Eagle Claw. And it was a disaster, wasn't it?"

In those days before CNN and the Internet, few seventh graders read the newspaper or watched the six o'clock evening news. So one day Mr. Snyder showed us a newsreel film about the botched operation: We learned how the U.S. aircraft sent to rescue the hostages had collided with each other and burned in the Iranian desert.

Discussions about the hostage crisis naturally segued into discussions about the upcoming U.S. presidential election. As Mr. Snyder had repeatedly noted, President Carter's approval ratings had fallen as low as 28 percent. His administration was under siege not only from the Iranians, but also from the flagging economy.

All that made the victory of Ronald Reagan more likely. And with the election only days away, this was a hot topic in class.

I had no real grasp of current political topics like supply-side economics, East-West détente, and stagflation, of course. My parents were both Republicans; and in classroom discussions I supported Ronald Reagan out of a vague sense of parental loyalty.

This was one of the few topics about which Bobby and I disagreed. Out on the playground one day, he had solemnly informed me that he was a Democrat and would be rooting for Jimmy Carter. When I asked why, he merely kicked up a little clod of dirt and said, "My old man is a Democrat."

But on this day, it appeared that Mr. Snyder would not be

discussing either theology or current events. Taking my seat, I noticed the exotic-looking words that the teacher had written on the chalkboard: *Samhain*, *Crom Cruach*, and *Bwca Llwyd*.

"All right," said Mr. Snyder. He was a tall, thin man in his mid-thirties who had gone prematurely bald. He had a brown mustache that the more ironically inclined students often likened to a caterpillar. "We're going to take a break from our usual flow of topics. Since Halloween is this Friday, I thought it might be a good day to talk about the origins of the Halloween holiday. And it does relate to church history, in some ways that might surprise you."

I surreptitiously swiveled around in my desk so that I could steal a glance at Leah. She was seated two rows over from me. When I saw her I felt my heart flutter, as they say—and even at the age of twelve I had enough self-awareness to feel a little silly for this. As I've mentioned, I had been looking at her for all of my life.

After wearing her blonde-brown hair straight for years, Leah had of late begun wearing it in the feathered hairstyle that celebrities like Farah Fawcett and Jaclyn Smith had recently made all the rage. She had grown a few inches, too, so that we now stood more or less eye-to-eye. (My pubescent growth spurt, which would eventually bring me to my present height of 6'1", would begin the following summer; but I had no idea of this at the time.) Leah's legs were long, tanned, and lightly muscled.

She was by no means the prettiest girl in the St. Patrick's junior high. But she could easily be counted among the most attractive ones; and I grew more than a little anxious whenever I saw other boys talking to her—especially the taller, stronger, and more aggressive boys in the eighth grade.

"Halloween," Mr. Snyder began, "was originally a Celtic holiday in the British Isles, known as *Samhain*. The Celts celebrated Samhain after the fall harvest. Samhain represented the end of the growing season, and the beginning of the darker time of the year."

I was mildly disappointed. Halloween a mere "harvest holiday"? The beginning of winter? So what? But Mr. Snyder was far from done.

"Of course," he continued, "there was a lot more to it than that. This is a spooky time of year, isn't it? Have you ever noticed that?"

I involuntarily nodded, and felt a little chill. I remembered the figure whom Leah, Bobby, and I referred to as "the ghost boy"; and I wondered if we would see him during our walk home today.

"The ancient Celts believed," Mr. Snyder said, "that this season at the end of the traditional harvest, between the autumnal equinox and the winter solstice, was a liminal time." Mr. Snyder paused, realizing that he had used a word beyond the range of the average twelve year-old vocabulary. "That means a time when the barriers between the world of the living and the world of the dead break down, or at least grow very thin. The Celts believed that the post-harvest holiday of Samhain was a time when the souls of the recently departed returned to their earthly homes, to visit their loved ones."

Now I definitely felt the chill. I had been but a small boy when my grandfather and grandmother Schaeffer had died. My memories of them were fragmentary at best. If what the Celts believed was correct, then maybe they still visited us from time to time—perhaps on one night per year, perhaps more often than that. This thought was simultaneously comforting and unsettling.

Mr. Snyder talked on, and told us how the Celtic festival of Samhain had been co-opted by the Catholic Church, and transformed into the holiday known as All Saints Day or All Hallows. The modern Halloween, he explained, was actually a truncated form of "All Hallows Evening", or the night before All Saints Day.

Then he told us how the jack-o'-lantern had been originally carved from a turnip, and then a gourd, and finally a pumpkin. The jack-o'-lantern was once thought to ward off evil spirits.

But by now I was only half-listening, my mind wandering off onto other topics. I was reflecting on the fact that I had never had a girlfriend before. I was enumerating Leah's qualities: Not only was she pretty—she was smart; she had the second-highest average in math so far this year, and seemed to breeze through every class discussion in our other courses, always prepared, always knowing the right answer.

I was wondering (for what might have been the millionth time) how many other boys had noticed her by now. How long would I have to make my move? I needed to ask her to "go with me"—as we said in those days.

That would require a previously unknown level of courage for me; I knew I wasn't up to it yet. How shattered I would be if she said no—that she "only liked me as a friend".

And, of course, with the walk home only a few hours away, I was also thinking about the ghost boy.

At 3:10 p.m. I met up with Leah and Bobby at the western edge of the school grounds, where Shayton Road bisected Ohio Pike. The latter road would, if followed west, take the traveler into the posh old-money eastern suburbs of Cincinnati, and after that, into the city itself.

Shayton Road was a two-lane highway that cut through farmland, pockets of residential housing, and endless acres of woods. This was the route that the three of us followed home everyday.

And more recently, Shayton Road had become the road of the ghost boy, if that was indeed what he was.

On the way to our rendezvous point, I spied Matt Stefano smoking cigarettes in a distant copse of trees past St. Patrick's all-purpose athletic field and baseball diamond. I didn't believe that he had seen me. At any rate, he was otherwise occupied and I seemed to be off the hook for now.

When I arrived at the edge of Shayton Road, Bobby and Leah were already waiting for me. Before they saw me, I watched them interact: Bobby said something funny or sarcastic (which I could not hear), and Leah playfully punched him on the shoulder.

This sort of interaction between them would have passed unnoticed by me two years earlier. But things were different now, and I felt a little pang of jealousy, followed by stabbing feelings of guilt. Bobby was my friend, right? Right—of course he was. But I nevertheless wished that he had gone on by himself, and left me alone with Leah.

"Hey, Schaeffer!" Bobby called out, having seen me. I hoped that he wouldn't mention my earlier humiliation at the hands of Matt Stefano. Not with Leah around.

"Yo," I said perfunctorily.

"You look kind of down in the dumps," Leah said, beaming. How had it gone unnoticed by me all those years when we were just kids, playing kickball and riding bikes around our neighborhood—how vivacious and lovely Leah would become?

"I'm okay," I said.

"Jeff had a rough day," Bobby began, until I cut him off with a sharp glance.

"What?" Leah inquired.

"Nothing," Bobby said quickly, understanding dawning on his face.

"That's right," I said. "Nothing."

"Hey," Bobby added. "Every day at school is a rough day for Schaeffer here because he's not exactly the smartest kid in the school, you know?"

Leah made a face at him. "Look who's talking. Okay. Fine—whatever. I have the feeling that there's something the two of you aren't telling me; but if you want to have boy secrets, be my guest. Come on, let's get going. I've got a lot of homework to do."

"Only you, Leah Carter, would rush home to do your homework," Bobby teased.

We walked for a while, leaving the school behind us and passing through a section of Shayton Road that was mostly wooded lots, and the occasional farmhouse. The subdivision where Leah and I lived was maybe a mile up ahead.

Yes—there *was* a school bus at our disposal, and we could have ridden home. This was 1980—not 1930 or 1950. But riding the school bus meant an extra hour of travel time, due to the way the route was configured. We therefore walked home whenever weather permitted.

We had walked not far at all when Leah broached the subject of trick-or-treat. The idea of going out for "one last Halloween" had arisen spontaneously among the three of us several weeks ago, and Leah had seemed enthusiastic about the prospect at the time. Her next words led me to wonder if she might not be on the verge of backing out.

"Are the other kids in our class going out trick-or-treating this year?" she asked.

"I'd say about half and half," Bobby answered. Bobby's assessment was probably accurate, more or less. "Why?"

Leah shrugged, hitching her backpack higher on her back. "No reason."

Of course there had been a reason, though. And while I was willing to let the matter drop, Bobby wasn't.

"Should we take a—*what do they call it*—a survey, Leah? Would you feel better about going out trick-or-treating if you found out that Brian Hailey and Sheila Hunt were going, too?"

This remark caused Leah's face to turn red, ever so slightly. Brian Hailey was the likely captain of the basketball team, an all-around athlete since little league. Most of the girls in the seventh grade had a crush on him. Leah probably had a crush on him, too.

Sheila was his female double, more or less. Little Miss Popular. All the boys had noticed her, whispered shyly about her on the playground. The girls, meanwhile, were divided: between struggling to imitate her and hating her.

"Bobby, Bobby, Bobby," Leah said, shaking her head. To my surprise, Leah was smiling. Bobby's remark had sounded fairly nasty to me; but Leah had found it endearing, apparently. "Never mind: We're going trick-or-treating. My mother has already made my costume. I'd never hear the end of it if I changed my mind now."

"There he is," I said. I was secretly glad to put an end to their all-too-cozy banter. But there was more to it than that: The ghost boy was here today—as he had been about two out of every three days over the past week or so. We were still a comfortable distance away from him. But we would have to pass by him in order to make it home.

He was sitting where he always sat: on a fallen log beside a stagnant pond that formed the pit of a little bowl of land alongside Shayton Road.

The pond was not a proper pond, really, but rather a low point where rainwater had collected. The depression in the land had been the site of an old industrial building, a structure that had once been a slaughterhouse (so the rumors went), or maybe just a warehouse. In any event, the building had been very old, and had been vacant for a long time when it was finally demolished two years earlier.

Now all that was left here was a barren crater filled with miscellaneous debris, and a shallow pool of water. The scene looked vaguely like something from a war zone. A bomb might have landed on the now nonexistent building, rather than a crew of demolition workers and a backhoe.

The crater was inaccessible for all practical purposes: It was hemmed in by two steep, slippery-looking hillsides behind it, and a sharp drop-off at the edge of Shayton Road on the near side. We had never played in the depression, never seriously thought about exploring the banks of the sludgy pond. This place was foul and muddy; and venturing down there would have meant a twisted ankle, if not a broken leg.

The crater had never attracted our notice much at all—until the ghost boy had begun appearing there.

He was wearing what he always wore: an old army fatigue jacket, jeans, and beat-up sneakers. The ghost boy might have been fourteen or fifteen years old—a few years older than us. He was smoking a cigarette and watching us approach. Doing, once again, what he always did.

I tried to look for his reflection in the pond and couldn't see it, though a skeptic could have easily claimed this was a result of the position of the boy, the pond, and the angle at which we approached him.

What was more difficult to explain was the way the kid seemed to blend into the hillside behind him—a craggy, muddy incline of dirt boulders and scrub pines. We had all noticed this: it was as if he were alternately there and not there.

"Maybe we should just ignore him," Leah said. We were drawing close now, though still just beyond earshot. "Maybe if we ignore him, then he'll ignore us."

Bobby snorted. "Fat chance. He doesn't want to be ignored. We've tried ignoring him before, haven't we? But he always calls out to us."

Leah nodded. "That's true. But you know—I was thinking: He could be a dropout from Youngman. Or—maybe he's already graduated. We've been scaring ourselves—telling ourselves that he's some kind of a vampire or a ghost or something. But maybe he's nothing more than an ordinary smartass, and we're psyching ourselves out."

"No," I said. "There's something about him that—isn't right. I don't know exactly what it is; but there's something strange."

"Don't look at me, Leah," Bobby said. "I think I'm with Schaeffer on this one."

There *was* something about this kid that wasn't right. And it was more than his appearance. This kid *knew* things about each of us— knowledge that a stranger could not possibly possess in such an offhand manner. But the only secrets he mentioned were the ones that we were ashamed of.

One day the boy had asked Leah, *"Hey, you—blondie! What happened to your sister's favorite doll? Two summers ago. You know—that one she really liked."*

This had meant nothing to Bobby and me, of course. After we passed by the boy that day, though, we had noticed that Leah's face had turned pale. "He knew," she said. "I don't know how; but he knew."

When we asked her to elaborate, Leah recounted a quarrel with her sister, Katie, from two summers ago. Katie had an antique doll that she practically loved; it was not only rare and unique, it was also a family heirloom that had belonged to their grandmother.

"I was so mad at Katie that day," Leah explained, "that I went into her room and stole the doll from her dresser drawer. I knew where she kept it. Then I threw the doll in the trashcan out by the curb. About an hour later I felt bad about what I'd done, and went to retrieve it. But by then the garbage truck had already collected the trash." Leah hung her head. "Several days passed before Katie discovered that the doll was missing, and I played dumb. I've never told anyone about what I did. I still feel lousy about it."

On another occasion, the ghost boy had asked Bobby, "Hey you, the tall one in the middle. Yeah, you: Why do you hate your dad so much?"

This had provoked an angry reaction in Bobby, and Leah and I had had to restrain him, to keep him from plunging down the dangerous embankment between the road and the pond.

"Don't listen to that guy," I'd said. "He's just talking and making random guesses. He doesn't know anything about us."

But of course, the boy *had* known things about us—he'd known about Leah's secret disposal of the heirloom doll, which would have been virtually impossible for a stranger to have conceived through random guesswork.

Today, I would discover, I was the ghost boy's chosen target. We walked by the edge of the depression, trying our utmost to ignore him, and he said:

"One of you has a secret today!"

Bobby gave him the finger. "Shove off, dickhead. We're not buying into your crap today."

The ghost boy leaned back on his log and took a long, thoughtful drag on his cigarette. For a brief second, I could have sworn that I saw solid earth and trees through his body; and then that illusion was gone. He was all there again—unusually pale and odd in any number of ways, but there.

"Oh, a tough guy, huh?" the ghost boy challenged. "Well, I'll let you go today. After all, you hate your father, even if you won't admit it to yourself."

"Don't listen to him, Bobby," I cautioned. "He's only trying to get a rise out of you. Like before."

"Oh, ho, ho. A peacemaker, are you?" he asked, addressing me.

"Well, it just so happens that you're the one who has a secret today. Imagine that."

This made me immediately nervous, because I knew that I *was* harboring secrets. I was feeling differently about Leah than I ever had, and I didn't yet know how to tell her so. Although Bobby was my friend, I was no longer content to have us hanging around as a three-some all the time. I wanted Leah to myself.

I didn't know how the ghost boy could have known any of this, but I was almost certain that he grasped my innermost thoughts. He had done no less in the cases of Leah and Bobby, after all.

That wasn't a conversation I was prepared to have. Almost without thinking, I knelt and picked up a rock. Then another.

The ghost boy smiled. In a voice that was a few octaves deeper than his normal adolescent boy's voice, he said, "Go ahead, try it."

So I threw both rocks. The results of that effort were almost as strange as the ghost boy's impossible knowledge.

"Come on," I said to Leah and Bobby. "Let's get out of here."

Simultaneously, we all resumed walking, quickening our pace to double time. Leah and Bobby had seen what I had seen, hadn't they?

Our one lucky break was that there was a bend in the road directly beyond the pond. We didn't stop our forward march until we were well on the other side of that bend, and beyond visual contact with the ghost boy.

Leah said, breathing heavily, "Tell me you guys didn't see that, okay? I need to believe that was just my imagination playing tricks on me." She stopped, unslung her backpack, and allowed it to drop at the side of the road. "So tell me that guys, okay?"

Bobby shook his head slowly. "If that was your imagination, then my imagination was doing the same thing. What about you, Schaeffer?"

I might have been visibly trembling now. Probably I was. "I saw it. I don't know what to call it, but—"

"Just stop! Okay?" Leah shouted. "Can we just forget about it, already?"

Bobby looked at Leah, at me, and then back at Leah.

"Sure," he said. "Let's just forget about it. We don't have to talk about it, do we, Schaeffer?"

"Nope. Nothing we need to talk about."

"Okay then," Leah bent down and hoisted her backpack again. We resumed walking.

In another ten minutes we reached the Shayton Estates subdivision, where Leah and I both lived, but on separate streets. Built on converted farmland back in '77, Shayton Estates represented the march of suburbanization into Withamsville. Bobby lived farther down Shayton Road, in a little rundown farmhouse that he shared with his mother, and a dog named Bluebell.

"See you later," Leah and I both called after him, as we made the turn onto the main road of our subdivision.

"Later," Bobby said, not looking back, but casting up a single hand in salutation.

Alone with Leah now, I felt that I needed to somehow maximize this time alone with her. But what could I say?

I naturally said the wrong thing.

"Listen, Leah," I said. "If—if that bothered you back there, we don't have to go trick-or-treating Friday. It's okay."

She stopped in the middle of the road.

"I don't mind going trick-or-treating. Didn't I already say that I'm going to go? I simply don't want to talk about—that—*other thing* again. *Okay?*"

"Okay," I said. Jeez, I thought.

"Listen, Jeff: I'm sorry. But I don't want to talk about that ghost boy anymore. Got it? And from now on I'm riding the bus home. At least tomorrow, anyway."

"Okay, Leah," I said. "You have a good night."

"Have a good night, Jeff."

We had reached Leah's street, and she turned toward her house. After that exchange, I wasn't about to offer to walk her home (although I would *very much liked* to have done that).

The ghost boy had clearly upset Leah. He had upset me too, for that matter—and not only with his embarrassing secrets.

The rocks that I threw at the ghost boy had both found their mark, almost by accident. (In truth, it had been my intention for them to merely land close by, perhaps splattering him with mud.)

The ghost boy did not attempt to evade the projectiles, nor did he raise a hand in reflex, as most people would.

Leah, Bobby, and I had all watched in silent amazement as the rocks passed through the body of the ghost boy.

And when each rock passed through him, the ghost boy changed. For a split second he was no longer a boy at all: he was a rotting corpse with exposed rib bones, a grinning skull trailing remnants of long hair.

It was as if the rocks had broken whatever energy field sustained the illusion of an actual boy. That was the explanation I would give myself in the years to come, as I reflected back on that day by the little pond, when I threw rocks to avoid the revelation of uncomfortable secrets.

Those thoughts would become the reflections of a much older man, who could look back on the actual events with a certain degree of detachment. At the time, I pushed the few seconds of the nightmarish vision to the back of my mind. Truth be told, I was at that juncture more concerned with Leah: What would it take for me to move past my fear and make us more than "just friends"?

In a more normal year, my crush on Leah might have remained the defining event of the season. But Halloween of 1980 was to be a time of strange sightings for the three of us. And we hadn't seen the last of them yet. In the very near future, it would be impossible for me to avoid confronting them.

4

B obby, Leah, and I had coordinated our Halloween costumes
to a certain degree. Bobby and I were both going out dressed
as pirates. Leah would be dressed as an Indian princess, or
Native-American female royalty, as they would say in the politically
correct parlance of the twenty-first century. (Leah's costume would be
controversial today; but it wasn't in 1980.)

In past years my costumes had covered all manner of Halloween
themes, a few of which made my twelve-year-old self cringe: At eight
I had been *Casper the Friendly Ghost*. Then the inevitable *Star Wars*
stormtrooper and Darth Vader.

My pirate costume struck me as a fitting choice for a twelve-
year-old boy who was embarking on his last Halloween outing. It
wasn't much of a costume at all, in the technical sense: I'd located a
buccaneer hat, an oversized belt with a fake gold buckle, and a
plastic sword and scabbard at K-Mart. I'd also wear a white shirt
and a pair of funky baggy pants that were already part of my normal
wardrobe. Had I known about the future Johnny Depp movie, I
would have considered my costume to be very *Pirates of the
Caribbean*-esque

My father was of a different mindset. To him, all this Halloween foolishness was something that I should have left behind with true childhood—at the age of nine or ten, perhaps.

He happened to walk by my room that night after dinner, as I was trying on my costume before the mirror, checking how I would look on Halloween night. Ordinarily I wouldn't have cared so much. But I would be spending the evening with Leah. I didn't want to look like a total dweeb.

"My son the pirate," he said, stepping into my room.

The remark hadn't been delivered with any degree of harshness. My father seldom raised his voice. At the age of twelve, I could recall being spanked only a handful of times—and by now most of those memories were distant. Spanking and yelling weren't my father's style. He had more subtle ways of expressing his disapproval. And I never failed to respond to it.

"This'll be the last year," I said. As I may have mentioned, we had had versions of this conversation before.

My father nodded. "My last Beggars' Night was in nineteen forty-seven. I was nine years old. It was also only my third Beggars Night, you know, because they suspended the practice during the war. No one had time or resources for trick-or-treating during the war."

There he went, talking about his childhood during World War II as if it were only yesterday. The year I turned twelve, my father was already forty-two, making him about a decade older than the fathers of most of my classmates.

I loved my dad, but at times he seemed more like a grandfather than a father, a visitor from another time and place.

Not only did he talk endlessly about distant events that had no relevance to my life, he also used unnecessarily antiquated language when the mood struck him. "Beggars' Night" was an old timer's word, more or less peculiar to Ohio, for what everyone else referred to as Halloween or trick-or-treat. *Hello, Dad, it's 1980*, I felt like saying—but didn't.

"Have you given any more thought to my suggestion?" he asked.

His suggestion, of course, had been more than a suggestion—it had been a subtle form of pressure. This year my sister, Carrie, turned seven—an age my father believed to be far more appropriate for trick-or-treating. Since October 1st Carrie had been breathlessly enthusiastic about the prospect of trick-or-treat, marking off the days on our kitchen calendar. But at seven she was too young to go out trick-or-treating alone. Even in 1980.

Under ordinary circumstances, the task would have fallen to one, or both, of my parents. But of course, this wasn't an ordinary year. My mother was recovering from a sprained ankle. One morning in September she had gone out to prune her knockout roses in preparation for the autumn, when she'd slipped on the front step and taken a nasty fall. A neighbor had found her lying on the front walkway and called an ambulance. Mom turned out to be all right (minus the sprained ankle) but walking long distances would be out of the question for her for the foreseeable future. She was still hobbling around the house on crutches.

"I wouldn't mind taking your sister out," Dad said. "But several of our big clients have their fiscal year closings on October 31st. You know what that means."

Of course I knew what that meant. My father was a mid-level accountant at a Cincinnati accountancy office. "Closing" meant a final tally and accounting of the year's books for each of the firm's corporate clients.

That usually meant a week of brutally late nights for my dad and his colleagues, right up to and including the night of the closing itself.

"And I wouldn't mind taking her out, either," I countered as tactfully as I could. "But Bobby and Leah and I have been planning this for weeks now. It's our last Halloween."

The truth—which I could never have confided to my father—was that I wouldn't have minded skipping the outing with Leah and Bobby, and accompanying my sister instead. Then I imagined Bobby and Leah out at night, walking the streets. It would be almost like a date, wouldn't it? And it had seemed to me that the two of them had been growing rather flirtatious of late. Bobby was my friend; and Leah was my friend—and that was the problem. Neither one of them owed me anything. If those two ended up getting together, I could make no case for betrayal. I had no claim on Leah.

"Okay," Dad said. "I'm not going to order you to cancel on your friends and take your sister out. But someday, son, you're going to have to learn what it means to step up to the plate when others need you. That's a lesson I had to learn at a young age. Your mother and I have tried to make things easier on you. We never wanted you to struggle. But sometimes I wonder if we've made you a little too self-centered."

I could easily predict what was coming next. My father had been too young for either World War II or Korea, but he had been a Cold War draftee in the late 1950s. He had reenlisted once in order to raise money for college.

My dad had been in the army during the Cuban Missile Crisis of 1962. Stationed in West Germany at the time, he'd been given a fallout suit and an M14 rifle, and told to expect a tactical nuclear strike and an invasion from the east should the crisis escalate into war. All the while, he would have to face the possibility that his friends and loved ones back home had been vaporized by Soviet missiles fired from Cuba.

In my more contemplative adolescent moments, I was able to acknowledge that yes, my father's growing up years had been more difficult than mine had been (*so far, anyway*). But my concerns were mostly limited to what remained for me in junior high, and high school beyond that.

And Leah.

"You don't think you'll be done with closing by Halloween night?" I asked.

My father was leaving the room.

"I don't know, son. If I can, I'll finish up and be home in time to take your sister out. Otherwise, Carrie will have to stay home while her big brother goes out."

5

I n case you're wondering, yes—I was feeling like a heel. I didn't have to ask what my father would have done at the same age, because I already knew: He would have put his own interests aside and taken care of others.

I knew that I wasn't martyr material, and I also knew that I was self-absorbed. But this realization didn't give me any magical power over my self-absorption. All I could think about was Leah and Bobby going out Friday night, possibly holding hands, possibly (and this thought really needled me) sharing a goodnight kiss at the end of the evening. Bobby, I recalled, had already claimed to have gone to "second base" with Molly Evans, a seventh grader who attended Youngman. I didn't like to think about him going to second base with Leah—or even first base, for that matter.

I went to St. Patrick's the next day with a lot on my mind: my conflicted feelings about Leah and Bobby, my mortal terror of Matt Stefano, and my guilt over what amounted to my refusal to do as my father asked. I was a duplicitous, disloyal friend. I was an undutiful son and brother. And I was clueless when it came to girls.

I was also beginning to examine what I had seen at the pond the previous day. There could be no doubt about what the ghost boy had turned into. Although we had not yet discussed it among ourselves, Leah and Bobby had seen the flash of the withered corpse, too. The real ghost boy.

Someday, I knew, I would have to think about what that meant. It surely had implications for my larger view of the world. I decided, however, that such an analysis could wait.

It was Wednesday. I had no idea what was coming my way in about forty-eight hours, on Halloween night.

When I arrived in my homeroom, the first thing I noticed was that Bobby's seat was empty. When he didn't show up for first period, I finally broke down and asked our homeroom teacher, Mrs. Durr, who also happened to teach first period science. She informed me that Bobby's mother had called him in sick.

Bobby was by no means the sickly type, though the occasional out-of-school sick day wasn't beyond him. I wondered: Had he been disturbed by what we had seen at the pond? *More disturbed than he had let on, perhaps?*

During the morning break and the lunch hour I did my best to avoid Matt Stefano. To my pleasant surprise, the rogue eighth grader didn't seek me out. Maybe he had found another target. Maybe he had forgotten me.

During the post-lunch break I participated in a H-O-R-S-E game with some of the other seventh grade boys at the basketball hoop at the front of the primary school building. When I could, I snuck glances at Leah: Seventh grade was the year that the girls in our class stopped playing jump rope and hopscotch during recess and started actively gossiping. I saw Leah in the middle of a group of the other girls. I didn't dare walk up to her—not with all those other girls around, and not after yesterday.

I did make it my business, though, to coincidentally reenter the school building at the same time as Leah at the end of the lunch break.

"Did you know that Bobby is out sick today?" I asked her. There were two seventh grade homerooms at St. Patrick's. Leah was in the other one, so she might not have been aware of Bobby's absence.

Leah rolled her eyes. That could have been a good sign, and it could have been a bad one. "Bobby is probably playing hooky. That's Bobby for you."

"Well, the two of us can still walk home tonight, right?" I asked. I wondered if I sounded as desperate as I felt. Hadn't Leah said yesterday that she would take the bus home today?

"I told you, Jeff: I'm riding the bus. No way I'm walking by that freaky kid again."

"What do think that really was?" I asked her. "What he really was —or *is*?"

"Jeff, I don't want to talk about it. I thought I'd made that clear."

With that she separated herself from me, and headed for her homeroom. I had been doing a lot better with Leah *before* I decided that I liked her, I now realized.

At the end of the day, I toyed with the idea of riding the bus home with Leah. She certainly hadn't invited me—not that I needed her invitation; I had as much right to ride the bus home as she did. But my presence on the school bus would not go unnoticed by her, and it might send the wrong signals.

Did Leah realize that I "liked" her? I had by now concluded that she must have at least a vague idea, some inkling. Leah was a sharp girl, after all, and I'd been acting differently around her of late. Heck, I'd been acting differently when I was by myself, inside my own head, for that matter.

The previous summer I'd heard, for the first time, that old Four Seasons song, "Walk Like a Man." The moral of the song seemed to be that if you tried too hard to show a girl that you liked her, then you came off as desperate, and actually ended up driving her away. The full how and why of this were as yet too foreign and complicated for me to grasp, but I did grasp the general concept.

I therefore decided to walk home that day by myself; and would later wonder (I still wonder) if I could have prevented everything that followed by simply riding the bus home. I've been contemplating this question for well over thirty years, and I'm no closer to the answer than I was in October of 1980.

When the 3 p.m. bell sounded I walked outside, past the rumbling school buses that were all lined up at the parking lot exit that emptied into the four-lane highway, Ohio Pike. That road, also known as State Route 125, is a very old road. Its eastern half is built atop the path of a nineteenth-century horse and wagon route; and sections of it are said to be haunted. But those are other stories that will have to wait until another time.

Directly across from the school was a little pony keg and convenience market called The Village Market. It wasn't one of those slick franchise places, but an independently owned establishment that had been there since the early 1960s, at least.

It was a warm day, and I felt more than a little thirsty. I decided, half on a whim, to cross the highway to the Village Market and treat myself to a cold Coke or a Pepsi. This wasn't a normal indulgence for me, but I was feeling self-indulgent at the moment. Or so I told myself. I knew that this would also give me a chance to walk by bus number 55, the one that Leah would have already boarded. Maybe she would see me and change her mind. Maybe.

I waited at the crosswalk. I was disappointed to see bus 55 roll past me when the light changed, presumably with Leah still aboard. I couldn't see her, and I didn't dare try to spot her face behind one of the bus's sun-reflecting windows. If she had changed her mind and decided to walk home with me, she would have presented herself by now.

The crosswalk flashed WALK, and I started across the highway with a group of two or three other students. The Village Market received a lot of business from the St. Patrick's afterschool crowd, and it was probably the grade school's only real off-campus "hangout". The St. Patrick's administration tolerated the Village Market's status uneasily; there was something vaguely unseemly about an establishment that sold beer, cigarettes, and soft-core skin magazines like *Playboy*. (The latter were stored discreetly behind the counter.) But there wasn't much the school administration could do about the place.

Having reached the other side of the highway, I once again made a wrong turn. I should have followed the other students into the

Village Market without looking at the old man with no legs who sat in the wheelchair beside the ancient maroon Oldsmobile. I should have averted my eyes and kept walking.

Or maybe I should have gone over to him, and did what he asked. Maybe that would have changed the outcome, broken the chain of events that I would later come to regard as the "curse".

I was already trailing behind the others when he caught my attention, my thoughts bouncing among their recent mélange of topics. He was a very old man, dressed in old green work pants, a stained button-down dress shirt faded to an indistinguishable color, and the sort of round-rimmed dress hat that men had stopped wearing several decades ago.

And he was beckoning to me.

He extended his hands in a gesture that was simultaneously a supplication and a command.

"Come here, boy!" he croaked. "I need your help."

That was when I also noticed the pile of groceries at the base of his wheelchair. The man had apparently made a purchase in the Village Market. Then while wheeling out to his car, he had lost control of the bag. The split brown paper sack had disgorged its contents onto the gravel: a plastic bottle of milk, a few canned goods, and several other packages that I could not distinguish.

I started to do as he asked. Turning decisively away from the market's entrance now, I walked toward him.

It might have been only my imagination—though subsequent events would convince me that there had been more than my imagination at work. As I drew closer to the shriveled, legless man, his face seemed to contort into something sinister and lupine. His nose seemed to grow sharper and more angular with each step of mine. His face elongated into something not quite human.

And inside that mouth that I had believed to be toothless, I saw— or could have sworn I saw—a row of canine incisors.

I flinched, my heart in my throat. I took a step backward.

Then he was just a harmless old man again.

"Help me," he pleaded. He pointed to the mess in the gravel, pleadingly. "I've dropped my things."

I continued to walk backward, without turning my back on the old man. I was afraid to help him. I was afraid to do what I would have previously believed to be the right thing. I was afraid of the risk it would have entailed.

In a different frame of mind, I might have chosen differently. I might have been able to write off the old man's momentary shift in appearance as an illusion. But this was coming on the heels of the ghost boy's hideous transformation yesterday. I was still confused about the reality of the situation; but I knew that I was not going to step within lunging distance of the old man in the wheelchair.

And anyway, I thought. How could the old man have driven here with no legs? The scene strongly suggested that he had arrived at the store in the maroon Oldsmobile—a Cutlass sedan that had probably rolled off the assembly line when JFK, or maybe even Ike, was in the White House. But how could the old man have driven it?

After a few more paces I turned my back on the man, and headed through the door of the Village Market.

I was immediately greeted by Gene, the proprietor of the Village Market. Gene was in his normal place behind the cash register. Gene was an older man who had jet-black curly hair (probably dyed) and the bulbous, blood-vessel cracked nose of a lifelong drinker. He was a tall, shuffling man who wore bifocals and "grandpa" sweaters. Gene spoke in slow, phlegmy syllables, punctuated by frequent coughs.

I don't think that I even returned Gene's greeting. I immediately said: "There's a man out in the parking lot who needs help. He has no legs."

"What?" Gene asked. He might have thought that I was talking about a recent accident victim.

I shook my head. "No. Not that. His legs have been—amputated. He's by his car in a wheelchair. He dropped his groceries."

If the man had indeed purchased goods in the Village Market, I would have expected recognition to dawn on Gene's face at this point. But Gene still seemed perplexed and maybe even a bit dubious of my story. He stepped from behind the counter and said: "Okay. I'll go check it out. Don't you kids steal anything."

This is the right thing to do, I thought, as Gene pushed open the sighing door of his store, and its little bell jingled. *Helping that old man wasn't my responsibility, after all.*

It seemed proper to wait for Gene to return, so I simply stood there. The St. Patrick's students who had crossed Route 125 with me were now beginning to queue at the counter with their purchases. The inside of the small, cramped store was cool from the electric beverage coolers that lined the walls. Some of the coolers contained beer, but the St. Patrick's students didn't bother with these, tempted though they might have been. Gene had been known to sell the occasional pack of cigarettes to a St. Patrick's eighth grader when no one was looking, but not beer. The *Playboy* magazines behind the counter were also strictly off-limits.

Gene walked back inside less than a minute after he had stepped out, shaking his head in mild frustration.

"There's no old man out there," Gene said. He took his accustomed place behind the counter and began typing the first of the student's orders into the cash register. He typed in each item manually, after looking at the code on the price tag. Barcodes existed in 1980; but Gene's was a small store and he had not yet adopted them.

"But," I protested. "He's driving an old car—an Oldsmobile. And he's in a wheelchair."

"Nope," Gene said, without looking at me. He announced the first student's total charges. "Take a look for yourself."

I did as Gene suggested. I leaned out the front door, and looked across the expanse of the Village Market's parking lot. I could see the adjacent business establishment (a seasonal fruit and vegetable market) and the row of trees behind the store. But there was no old man, and no maroon Oldsmobile.

Had he left? Had someone else helped him?

And then the thought that I didn't want to consider but had to: *Had he even been there at all?*

"I think you're a little crazy from the heat," Gene suggested, not unkindly. "Why don't you cool off with a Pepsi or something? I've got a sale running: thirty-five cents."

Not knowing what else to do, I did as Gene advised. I walked down the aisle along the far wall, across the green floor that always seemed to bear a light coating of dust and sticky residue. I opened the soft drink cooler and withdrew a can of Pepsi.

To my relief, the other St. Patrick's students were gone by the time I returned to the front of the store with my purchase. I wondered how much they had overheard of my exchange with Gene. If they were paying attention, I must have looked pretty silly.

Without further discussion of the old man, I paid for my Pepsi and stepped back outside into the golden yet slightly shadowy glare of the late October sun. It was that time of year, as Mr. Snyder had said, when the world was different.

I drained half of my Pepsi while waiting for the crosswalk. In order to walk home, I would have to cross the highway again and walk to the far end of the St. Patrick's parking lot, to the edge of Shayton Road.

I crossed Ohio Pike when the light changed and returned to the grounds of the St. Patrick's campus. That was when I made my second wrong turn of the afternoon—or my third, if you believe that I should have swallowed my pride and ridden the bus home with Leah.

It would be a twenty- to thirty-minute walk home—even without the distraction of banter with Bobby and Leah. Despite the heat, I was aware of the liquid I was ingesting as I gulped the last few swallows of Pepsi, and permitted myself an indiscreet burp in the mostly empty school parking lot.

I felt the beginnings of a call of nature. It was not too urgent yet; but carbonated beverages have always gone right through me. They still do.

I had better make a pit stop in the school's restroom before beginning the walk home, I decided.

There was nothing particularly spooky about the St. Patrick's school facilities. After seven years as a student, the entire campus had become routine to me. To the best of my knowledge, there were no urban legends surrounding the school itself—no murky rumors of the suicide of a troubled student on the school grounds, no classrooms that were reputed to contain odd drafts or disembodied voices.

Nevertheless, there was something vaguely discomforting and uneasy about the empty building on this particular afternoon. It wasn't even three-thirty yet. There were probably still a few teachers and students lurking about. But as I walked down the short flight of stairs that took me to the lower level of the junior high building, I could not help thinking about the ghost boy, and the mysterious old man. Were they down here waiting for me?

The boys' bathroom was deserted. I stood there at the urinal, doing my business, my imagination running wild. There was a row of three toilet stalls behind me. *I should have checked each one*, I thought, emptying my bladder. *I should have opened all three doors and looked inside.*

Finally done, I avoided looking in the mirror as I washed my hands. Weren't mirrors one of the favorite haunts of spiritual beings? I thought I had heard that in a movie once, or maybe read it somewhere.

I was drying my hands when someone came at me from the side nearest the door. I must have shouted *OOF!*, because the impact was abrupt and solid enough to practically knock the wind out of me.

A second later I found myself pinned up against a nearby wall. It wasn't the ghost boy or the man in the wheelchair.

It was Matt Stefano.

He gave me a quick, sharp punch in the stomach. For a second I thought that the Pepsi I'd purchased at the Village Market was going to come up and all over both of us. But it didn't.

"You caused me three demerits!" Matt said, in a low, deliberate growl. "I'm going to kill you."

As if to demonstrate his seriousness, Matt reached into his back pocket and withdrew a short, rectangular brown object. He flicked a black button on the face of the object and *whoosh!*—a silver, wicked-looking blade flipped out of its interior.

I now realized the stakes: I was alone in an enclosed space with a very pissed-off juvenile delinquent, and he had just pulled a switch-blade on me. While arguably more mundane, this situation carried an immediate threat that eclipsed the more unexplainable happenings of recent days.

If I had not just urinated, I am sure—even now—that I would have done so in my pants.

There was a sound of clattering just outside the restroom. Matt saw something in his peripheral vision. As suddenly as he had pinned me to the wall, Matt shoved me aside and closed the knife with one quick, practiced movement.

Barely a few seconds later, Mr. Larbus, the school janitor, wheeled a mop and bucket into the boys' bathroom. He pushed it in front of him, holding on to the handle of the mop.

Mr. Larbus had been whistling; but he stopped whistling once he took in both Matt and me. Matt had by now pocketed his weapon, and there was a physical distance between us that afforded the older boy a measure of plausible deniability. But Mr. Larbus must have read something in our body language—and surely he read something in my expression.

"Any trouble here?" Mr. Larbus asked. The janitor was in his early sixties, only a few years from retirement. During the Second World War, he had been taken prisoner by the Germans; and a Nazi interrogator had pulled out three of his fingernails, which had not grown back. He was an older man, yes; but a large man and not one to be trifled with.

"No trouble," Matt said. Stefano looked at me as if to say, *Say anything at all, and I'll kill you for sure.*

Mr. Larbus raised one eyebrow dubiously. "You sure about that?"

"He's sure," Stefano answered. "I mean: *We're* sure."

I took a moment to contemplate my options. Mr. Larbus was an adult. If I told him what had happened, he would take my side. On the other hand, though, as the school janitor he had no real authority over any of the students; and a half-hearted attempt at intervention on his part might only make things worse.

"I'm sure," I said at length. "Everything is fine."

"All right, then," Mr. Larbus said, clearly not believing either one of us. "Well, if the two of you are done in here, I need to mop the floor."

I waited as Matt stalked out of the restroom. I wanted to put as much distance between us as possible.

Mr. Larbus shook his head after Matt left—whether at the lie or the apparent bullying, I wasn't sure.

"Well?" he finally asked.

Taking my cue, I walked out. But instead of turning left, and walking up the stairs and out the main entrance of the school (which Matt would be expecting) I turned right instead. I passed through the double doors that led to the classroom area.

I walked down to my homeroom classroom. Mrs. Durr had gone for the day, so I had the whole room to myself. I sat in my usual homeroom seat, feeling ashamed and ridiculous. What was I doing here, but hiding from Matt Stefano?

When I stepped out of the front entrance of St. Patrick's about twenty minutes later, the shadows were already lengthening. By the last week of October in Ohio, the days are growing short.

The hour was probably heading for four o'clock; and I still had to make the walk home. I would have arrived a lot faster had I taken the bus with Leah.

There was no sign of Matt Stefano in the parking lot. I suppose that he felt no need to wait for me. After all, where was I going? He could exact his revenge tomorrow, or the next day.

When I reached Shayton Road I quickened my pace, in an effort to make up for lost time. My mother would be wondering where I was.

Then I approached the crater of the demolished warehouse, and the pond where the ghost boy habitually awaited us. *Please God*, I prayed silently, *let him not be there today. Whatever he is or isn't, let him not be there.*

But of course the ghost boy was there.

"Just you today, huh?" he called out. He was smoking that same cigarette, wearing the same faded army fatigue jacket, ratty pair of jeans, and sneakers.

I tried to ignore him, and walked faster. I would not look at him. It wasn't far to the bend, I told myself.

"*Come here, boy!*" the ghost boy called out. "*I need your help! I've dropped my things!*"

I froze. I realized that the ghost boy had repeated the words that the old man in the wheelchair had uttered, more or less verbatim.

I turned to look at him. The ghost boy smiled vindictively. For an instant, he gave me another glimpse of his other self—his true self.

"*For twelve hours you will know no peace,*" he croaked, in the voice of the old man. "*For twelve hours you will be tested. And you're weak. You won't survive.*"

"Go away!" I shouted, earnestly afraid now. And then I ran. The ghost boy laughed in my wake, his voice and demeanor that of an ordinary teenage hoodlum again. He might have been one of Matt Stefano's friends.

6

The next day during our morning recess, I gently chided Bobby for his sick day. Half jokingly, I asked him if the ghost boy had traumatized him into sickness.

But there was a more mundane explanation.

"That math test," he said. "I wasn't ready. I was home yesterday cramming."

We had indeed had a math test yesterday: The subject matter was complex fractions and decimals, standard seventh-grade math. Leah had finished the test twenty minutes before the end of the class. I was a little behind her, but I completed the exam by the period's end, and was reasonably confident that I had scored a middling B. That was more or less typical for me in math.

"Well, you and Leah are a whole lot smarter than me," Bobby said. "What do you want me to tell you?"

I didn't necessarily believe that this was true. Bobby displayed remarkable ingenuity when he wanted to, and a savviness that is called "street smarts" in the adult world. He was no dummy, even though his grades were far below mine—let alone Leah's.

But Leah's father was an engineer; and my parents were both certified public accountants. (My mother had taken an extended break from work upon the birth of my little sister. She would reenter the workforce years later, when Carrie started high school.) Leah and I came from educated, upwardly mobile households where education was emphasized, and good grades were expected. At the end of every semester, my parents spent a full hour going over my report card with me, praising me for my As, nodding at my Bs, and relentlessly questioning me over any Cs. A "D" or an "F" would have constituted a major disaster, and a cause for intense parental intervention.

Bobby's father, meanwhile, was absent from the home; and his mother was just trying to get by, working two jobs. No one cared about Bobby's grades. Not really.

I abruptly changed the subject, and told Bobby about what had happened yesterday: the old man in the parking lot, Matt Stefano, the vague threat that the ghost boy had shouted at me in the old man's voice. His reference to "twelve hours of being tested"—or something like that.

Bobby shook his head with a wry smile. "Schaeffer, I think you've been seeing things."

"What? You don't believe me?"

"Oh I believe the part about Matt Stefano. Absolutely. It's the other stuff that I'm a little—what's that word—*skeptical* about."

"But Bobby, you saw what that boy turned into the other day. "You even said that you saw it."

"I never said anything about what I saw," Bobby asserted. And come to think of it, I couldn't remember, with absolute certainty, whether Bobby had described the ghost boy's transformation—or explicitly confirmed that he had observed that horrible, momentary change.

But it had seemed pretty clear to me yesterday that my friends had seen what I'd seen. The shock had been unmistakable, written on their faces.

One of my friends, though, grew angry every time I raised the issue. My other friend was now apparently playing it "cool". Chafing against the unshielded credulity that we had all embraced in childhood, Bobby didn't want to admit that he had seen the "monster".

"What the ghost boy said," I continued. "It was almost like a curse."

"What if he isn't a ghost boy at all?" Bobby challenged. "What if he's just a boy who likes to yank other people's chains?"

"Then how could he know so much, about all of us, about your...?" I hesitated.

"How could he know that I have issues with my old man? Come on, Schaeffer: My home situation isn't exactly a big secret. There probably isn't a kid at either St. Patrick's or Youngman who knows me, who doesn't also know that my old man is basically no good."

"But what about Leah's secret?"

"What about it? She said it was a 'secret', but you know how girls talk. Maybe she told someone and forgot about it, or heck—anything is possible. When you break it all down, it's all pretty much Mickey Mouse stuff."

"Well, what that boy turned into wasn't Mickey Mouse."

"Who knows what you saw? What you really saw? I'm telling you man, that kid is just making some lucky guesses and playing with your mind. And as for 'curses'? The only curse on you is Matt Stefano. And you'd better watch out for him—because there might come a day when you run into him, and there isn't any Mr. Larbus, or Mr. Malinowski around. Or me, for that matter."

"Yeah, okay," I said. I didn't appreciate the fact that Bobby had so blatantly brought up his intervention in my Matt Stefano troubles, and how badly I had needed his help the other day.

"Anyway, about Leah."

"What about Leah?" I asked.

"You're kind of sweet on her, I think."

"I don't know. What if I am?"

Bobby shrugged. "What if you are?"

The unspoken question here was: *What if Bobby is "sweet on her" too?* That was a question that I didn't want to consider.

And I didn't have to—at least not at that moment. We both turned around at the familiar sound of the whistle summoning us back into class.

Nevertheless, the conversation had started me thinking along yet another line: I had recently felt pangs of conscience because I believed that I was, on some level, guilty of betraying my friend. But maybe I had been too quick to assume the best of intentions on Bobby's part. Perhaps he, too, had a self-serving agenda that involved Leah.

7

B obby and I walked home together that afternoon. Leah still insisted on riding the bus. Bobby had tried to coax her into walking with us, saying, "Come on, Leah," with that crooked smile of his. Leah refused, but I was dismayed to see that she smiled back at him, whereas she had reacted to me with such anger the other day.

While we were walking home, Bobby said, "I checked with Leah today. She's still on for tomorrow night. For trick-or-treat, I mean."

"Good," I replied in a neutral tone. For the past several days I had been avoiding Leah, whether out of damaged pride or fear of rejection I could not have said. Last year, Leah and I were much closer than she was to Bobby. However, Bobby seemed to have slipped into the vacuum that had recently been created by my temporary estrangement from her.

And it appeared that Bobby wasn't ready to let the matter drop.

"Man," he said, "you should have seen yourself blush today, when I asked you if you were sweet on Leah."

My response was immediate and emphatic. "I did not."

"Oh, yes you did, Schaeffer. You turned red as an apple. Red as a tomato. Red as—"

"Okay, okay. I get it." Since Bobby had brought the matter up, I decided that I had might as well pose the question that had been needling me.

"What about you? Do you have a thing for Leah?"

"Naw," Bobby said. "I'm going to go for Sheila Hunt."

This sounded to me like a deliberate, implausible evasion. Everyone in the seventh grade knew that Sheila Hunt and Brian Hailey were more or less an item, to the extent that is possible for junior high kids. Bobby would have had no chance with her.

We were coming up on the crater. I wondered what the ghost boy was going to say today—and what he was going to turn into. Would today be the day that he finally revealed all the secret resentments I'd been feeling toward Bobby?

The ghost boy, however, was nowhere to be seen. When we reached the pond, the ghost boy's log was unoccupied.

Bobby paused in the road, and cupped his hands to his mouth. *"Come out! Here we are! Come and get us!"* He punctuated this challenge with an obscenity or two. Then he started walking again.

"See?" Bobby said. "If the 'ghost boy' were a real ghost, then he wouldn't miss a day, would he?"

I shrugged, not wanting to open up that argument again. If Bobby wanted to believe that nothing had happened here, then let him believe that. Moreover, Bobby was right about one thing: Matt Stefano was a much more imminent threat to me than the ghost boy —or the unexplainable old man, for that matter—had ever been.

Looking back on it through the prism of middle age, I now realize that I would have been willing to do as Bobby urged me to do, and more or less write off the whole affair as an illusion. When we are young, we perceive and feel a lot of things that seem implausible and almost fantastical in later life. The older a man gets, the easier it becomes for him to doubt the perceptions of the twelve-year-old boy he once was.

And I would have been willing to second-guess myself, even then. But then the occurrences of the following night erased all room for second-guessing and doubts.

8

_____

Finally Halloween—and a Friday, to boot.

School that day was uneventful. Though I did see Matt Stefano, glaring at me from a distance several times, the eighth grader kept his distance. I thought more about his switch-blade: I wondered if Matt carried the weapon with him everyday, everywhere he went.

Leah was cordial to me, but distant, it seemed. Or maybe I was the one who was distancing myself from her. Not so long ago, the two of us were so comfortable with each other. And now we were so awkward.

Bobby and I walked home again that afternoon; the warm sunny weather promised good conditions for our outing tonight. It would be cool without being chilly, without any chance of rain.

The ghost boy was once again absent from his usual haunt. Maybe he's gone, I thought. Maybe he's finally gone; and maybe Bobby was right: It might all have been nothing more than a big psych-out.

"See you at quarter till seven," Bobby said, as I turned into the Shayton Road subdivision, and he kept walking down the main road. "At the corner of Wilma Court and Cider Mill Drive.

"I'll be there," I said. "Does Leah know where we're supposed to meet?"

"Don't worry about Leah," Bobby called over his shoulder. "She knows."

IT WAS GOING for six thirty when I finally finished adjusting my buccaneer hat and the rest of my makeshift pirate costume.

I stood before the mirror in my bedroom, looking at myself decked out as a pirate. My father had a point: I was a little too old for all of this; I looked ridiculous, in fact. I was already at that stage where I was seriously noticing girls and thinking about high school, and here I was, prepared to go walking around my neighborhood with a plastic sword.

This was an activity for kids, wasn't it? But I couldn't cancel on my friends now, less than an hour before I was scheduled to meet them. Nor did I have any intention of allowing Bobby to walk around all night alone with Leah, almost like two high school kids on a real date.

I took a moment to look around my room, and realized that the conflict that I had been having with my father was crystallized right here, even though there was no easy solution to it. I had recently started hanging up rock posters, which my father hated. My most recently acquired one, a promotional poster for Ozzy Osbourne's *Blizzard of Oz* album, struck a coincidentally Halloween-like theme. It featured the former Black Sabbath front man grasping a crucifix in a melodramatic seated pose, an animal skull and crouching cat on either side of him.

I had been too young for Black Sabbath's heyday ten years earlier, but Ozzy Osbourne's recent debut album was all the rage at St. Patrick's. With its screechy, dark lyrics and quasi-occult themes, the school's administrators all naturally hated it. So did my father, for that matter. *"Are you going to become a devil worshipper, son?"* he'd asked me when he'd first seen the poster, only half joking.

I assured him that no, that certainly wasn't the case, and that Ozzy Osbourne was really no different than Elvis and Chubby

Checker had been in his own day. But my father remained unconvinced. Elvis, for all his then controversial onstage gyrations, had later moved on to gospel music. "This guy is nothing like Elvis," my father had said. I dropped the argument, realizing that it was hopeless. My father, after all, had been almost thirty when America discovered the Beetles.

Even the tamer fare of my newly discovered youth culture provoked reactions of distaste from him. When he saw the cover of my Journey album, he remarked that lead singer Steve Perry looked "a lot like a woman." He then proceeded to ask if Steve Perry was "queer". I explained that no, no—Steve Perry actually had female groupies coming out the wazoo. Once again, the gap between the present and my father's cultural reference points was too vast. "This doesn't look like the sort of guy who gets a lot of women," he said. "But he might get a fair amount of attention from other men if he were in prison."

And so on.

On the other hand, my bedroom still contained artifacts of an earlier, simpler time when my father had found me a lot easier to understand. There were trophies from my little league days on the adjacent shelves, and my baseball card collection in two shoeboxes. Model fighter planes and bombers dangled from my ceiling, suspended almost invisibly by 10-lb. test fishing line. My dad had encouraged my interest in reconstructing military hardware in miniature. I could still recall the day—not all that long ago—when the two of us had hung those WWII Corsairs and Hellcats, along with the more modern Super Sabres and Phantoms.

Satisfied that I was as dapper as I was going to be in a pirate suit, I turned out the light in my bedroom and walked downstairs. My mother was about, still visibly limping from her ankle injury, but the first person I saw was Carrie, my seven-year-old sister.

"Hi, Carrie."

"Hi, Jeff."

Carrie was dressed as Tinker Bell. Her costume was comprised of a fairy frock of light green with gold and silver sequins, a set of diaphanous plastic wings on her back, and a little magic wand. The skirt of the costume was a bit too long for her, and hung down to her calves, instead of just above her knees.

She had been pacing about the kitchen, waiting for our father to get home. Dad had been, as anticipated, waylaid by work tonight, but he had told Carrie that he would make every effort to get home in time to take her out. Because in the end, her big brother hadn't come through on that one.

"Are you going out?" she asked, looking simultaneously hopeful and forlorn. She might have been wondering if, since my father was running late, I might not offer to take her along with Bobby, Leah, and me.

"Yes. With my friends from school."

"Oh. Okay."

"Dad will be home," I told her, as I walked out the door. "Dad will be home."

9

When I arrived at the place where Wilma Court and Cider Mill Drive intersect (those streets are still there, as far as I know), Leah and Bobby were waiting for me.

Leah looked breathtakingly pretty in her Pocahontas costume: It was about what you would expect: an imitation buckskin tunic and skirt, with lots of tassels and feathers. She had even put a little war paint on her face—possibly lipstick and eye shadow that had been repurposed for the occasion.

"Hi, Jeff," she said.

"Hi, Leah," I said. Did she know how pretty she looked? Did she know that *I* knew?

Bobby, meanwhile, seemed to be much more comfortable in his pirate costume than I was, although our two outfits were more or less the same. He somehow seemed to be more in character.

"*Hardy har har!*" he said, in a funny voice that made Leah smile. "*Last Halloween! Let's go score us some booty!*"

Trick-or-treat was just getting underway. There were kids walking among the houses, but not too many yet.

Most of them were significantly younger than us.

"Let's go, then," I agreed.

We saw nothing unusual for a while. I was more or less familiar with the houses that were close to the intersection of Wilma Court and Cider Mill Drive. A few of the neighbors even recognized Leah and me by name, though none of them recognized Bobby.

"Aren't you getting a little old for trick-or-treat, Schaeffer?" one of them asked me, in a joking manner that was not entirely a joke. This was Mr. Daley. He had been one of my little league coaches two summers ago.

"My last year," I told him. I almost asked him if he had been talking to my father. I'm twelve years old and I want one last trick-or-treat, I felt like saying. So shoot me.

"All right, then. Well, I hope you like Snickers."

"Everyone likes Snickers."

We were about halfway up Cider Mill when both the terrain and the houses grew more unfamiliar. I almost never had any occasion to walk so far in this direction; and this wasn't a route that I traveled often as a passenger in my father's car, either.

We were walking up the driveway of a house with a yard that was decorated by fake headstones, when Leah spoke out:

"Hey guys, look: Those gravestones aren't fake: They're *real*."

"What do you mean?" Bobby asked.

"Just look at them," she said.

There were lights on in the house, which I didn't recognize, but which seemed to be a perfectly normal suburban split-level with a brick and aluminum siding exterior. Nor was I initially suspicious of the headstones. These were common enough as Halloween decorations. They were usually made of plastic or Styrofoam, and bore clichéd epitaphs like "R.I.P." or "I'll be back!"

But as I looked closer, I saw that these particular ones were in fact different, somehow; and I could immediately see what Leah was talking about. I broke away from Bobby and Leah and stepped out into the lawn, toward the five gravestones.

"What are you doing, Schaeffer?"

"Hold on, Bobby," I said.

I crouched down in the grass, my plastic scabbard catching in the turf as I knelt.

The first headstone read,

Michael J. Hollis

1965 – 1978

"For what is seen is temporary, but what is unseen is eternal."
-2 Corinthians, 2: 18

"MICHAEL HOLLIS," I read aloud. "Wasn't he—?"

But of course we all knew who Michael Hollis was, if we thought about it for a moment. Michael Hollis had been a thirteen-year-old boy, a student at Youngman Elementary, who had been struck dead two summers ago when he rode his bike across Route 125 one day without bothering with the crosswalk, nor even with looking both ways. The accident had occurred just east of Withamsville, and the tragedy had hit the local community hard. Michael Hollis had, by all accounts, been a good kid who had simply made one careless mistake.

In the months following his death, Michael Hollis's fate had become a standard cautionary tale among local parents. Even my mom had invoked his name once or twice during the summer months, when children are especially prone to the illusion that they are unbreakable beings who will live forever: *"Be careful on your bike, Jeff; remember what happened to that Michael Hollis."*

Leah was kneeling beside me now.

"This isn't right," I said. "If this is someone's idea of a joke, well, it isn't funny."

Equally strange, though, was the headstone itself: It wasn't made from polyurethane, cardboard, or anything like that.

It was made from actual stone—probably granite. I touched the gray grave marker and felt not only its hardness, but its solidity as well.

"That couldn't be, could it?" Leah asked, as if reading my thoughts.

"No, it couldn't be," I replied. But the fact was that the gravestone of a recently deceased local teenager was here in this suburban front yard.

Without standing up, I moved laterally, away from Leah, to look at the next two gravestones. They were also for young people who had died recently. The first one, Diane Wallace (1964-1980) was another name that we all recognized. Diane Wallace had been killed in an automobile accident only two weeks after getting her driver's license. The inscription on the next gravestone, James Platt (1963-1977) didn't ring any bells; but if the pattern held, James Platt had probably been a local kid, too.

"Why?" Leah asked me. "Why would someone do this?"

"I don't know."

Bobby, in exasperation, had left the driveway and was now standing over us. "What?" he asked.

"You've heard of Michael Hollis, right?" I asked him.

Bobby paused to ponder the name.

"Yeah, the kid who got killed a few summers ago. He was riding his bike across the highway, right?"

"Right. Well, this gravestone has his name on it. What's more, this is a real gravestone, not a fake one that someone bought at Kmart."

I showed Bobby the other gravestones as well, and provided explanations for the one or two names that he didn't recognize.

Maybe this was another inevitable symptom of Bobby's comparatively loose upbringing: His single mother had little time to school him in the lore of the local kids who had met untimely ends, the ones who had crossed the street without looking, gone for a ride with the wrong driver, or perhaps consumed a fatal quantity of alcohol at a party. My parents, by contrast, were practically encyclopedias of these suburban examples of all that could go wrong for an adolescent.

"This is a pretty sick joke, then," Bobby said.

"Damn right," I said.

We were twelve-year-old boys, and reveled in various forms of black humor and sarcasm. But the irony conveyed by these head-stones was a little too black even for us. There was something fundamentally wrong here, we both knew.

And Leah was even more vocal in her disapproval.

"I say we skip this house," she said. She stood up. "I don't know who these people are, but I don't want any candy from them."

As if her declaration had summoned the occupants of the house, the front screen door creaked open. We all looked up.

"Do you kids want any candy or not?" the owner of the house asked us.

He wasn't what any of us would have anticipated. The home-owner was an early middle-aged man who wore a dress shirt and slacks—no tie. He might have been one of my father's colleagues at the accounting firm. Nor was he the slightest bit unfriendly. Quite the opposite, in fact.

"It looks like you're admiring our decorations. What do you think, kids? We really went all out this year."

A woman joined the man in the open doorway—his wife, obviously. Like her husband, she seemed to be the textbook example of normal. She was a moderately plump, blonde woman in her late thirties. Her hair was cut conservatively short and curled. She might have been one of my mother's friends, any one of the neighborhood women who my mom occasionally got together with to exchange local gossip or play bridge. (I didn't know most of their names, but I knew many of them on sight, and this woman somehow looked familiar.)

"We've got Milky Ways!" she beckoned. She held aloft a hollow plastic jack-o'-lantern filled with candy. Behind her, the warm light of a perfectly normal suburban home revealed an equally normal living room.

If we had been a few years older, we would have challenged them. We would have asked them why they had turned the deaths of local kids into warped Halloween clichés. But we were only twelve, and still very much accustomed to regarding adults as default authority figures. *(There were exceptions, of course: All of us—probably even Bobby —had received the standard lectures about the dangers of accepting rides from adult strangers.)* The couple seemed so nice, so solicitous, and none of us were able to summon the words to oppose them.

I don't remember which of us began walking toward the door first. Within about thirty seconds, though, all three of us were standing before the open doorway, holding open our candy bags so we could receive Milky Ways from Mr. and Mrs. Normal.

There was nothing odd about the exchange itself. We accepted our candy and thanked them. Each of us received one candy bar each, which was pretty standard this early in the evening. Later on, toward the end of trick-or-treat, homeowners would become more generous, giving each kid a handful of candy so as to avoid a large surplus of leftovers.

The only macabre element of the interaction came when the couple closed the door on us. The words of Mr. Normal—normal though he may have appeared—were a little bit "off".

"Be careful", he said. "It's a scary, scary night out there."

For some reason, that admonition sent a little chill up my spine, especially in light of the recent days' occurrences.

I was also mildly angry at myself. Those headstones on the front lawn—they were indecent, almost blasphemous. I should have said something, or questioned the couple, at the very least.

But I walked away from that front door without making the slightest gesture of protest. And what I saw next caused me to momentarily forget about the headstones.

A group of costumed children walked by, and there was a tall figure in the middle of them—perhaps a father who had been saddled with trick-or-treat duty for the evening. The lone man was not wearing a costume, of course. He was wearing a denim jacket.

Then I looked closer: the adult was not quite an adult, but a six-foot tall teenage boy named Matt Stefano. He wasn't actually with the children; that had been a temporary optical illusion. He was behind them, relative to where I stood; and with his faster pace he quickly moved past them.

He wasn't looking in my direction, thankfully; his gaze was fixed forward, as if something down the road had caught his attention.

Without looking down, Matt removed something from the pocket of his denim jacket. It was an object that I had seen before, and had never wanted to see again. I heard a click as the switchblade opened.

"Hey, that guy's got a knife!" one of the children said.

I hoped that this remark wouldn't provoke Matt. Although they were just little kids—compared to us—I really didn't know what Matt Stefano might be capable of.

Matt turned briefly and gave the group of children an evil smile that chilled me even more than the headstones had. But he kept moving. Although he had been turned in my direction for a few seconds, he luckily failed to notice me.

I now noticed that I was apart from my friends in the driveway. Bobby and Leah were still talking about the headstones, leaning over them and speculating.

"What's the matter, Schaeffer?" Bobby asked. "You look like you've seen another ghost."

Ordinarily a person would say, *You look like you've seen a ghost*. It is a testament to the oddities of that particular season that Bobby was able to meaningfully say "another ghost"—even though he had since come to disagree with me about the true nature of the ghost boy.

"Come on," Leah said. "Let's go. These people have a warped sense of humor, or something."

"It could be more than that," I began. "Those are real headstones. I've never actually priced one, but I imagine that they don't come cheap."

"Yeah, well—let's just forget about it."

I saw Bobby start to say something, and then he thought better of it. Bobby, like Leah, did not seem eager to discuss the possibility that the headstones had been more than a homeowner's sick prank. In the same way, neither of them had wanted to explore the possibility that the ghost boy might be more than just an ordinary teenage boy who had made some lucky guesses.

As we walked down the driveway toward the street, Leah allowed herself one last backward glance at the inexplicable headstones.

"Weird," she said. Yeah, it was weird, all right.

We made our way to the next house. It occurred to me that we were traveling, however slowly, in the same direction that Matt Stefano had been walking. That would be no problem, probably, so long as Stefano kept moving. But if Matt were detained for some reason, or decided to double back, we would run straight into him. And my pirate costume didn't much disguise me.

In that moment, I made a decision: It was one thing to back down from Matt Stefano when it was only the two of us—or even when Bobby was around, for that matter. But with Leah here tonight, the stakes were higher.

If I cowered before Matt Stefano tonight, Leah would lose all respect for me. And however much she liked me as a friend, I sensed that that would be the end of any chance that she might eventually like me as something more.

I didn't yet understand much about the whole amalgamation of masculinity, courage, and other factors that spurred female attraction. I only knew that being a coward before Matt Stefano would be the wrong thing to do.

I was therefore determined to stand up to him. But could I do that? I had never been able to do it before. Moreover, to view the matter objectively, Matt Stefano was older, larger, and stronger than me. To directly challenge him would be suicide—it would mean a bad beating, and maybe worse.

For the time being, I allowed myself to take comfort in the odds that we would not directly cross paths with him.

There were no headstones in the next yard. It was a normal looking split-level with an overgrown belt of shrubbery near the house, a white picket fence enclosing the back yard, and a tool shed in the back. There was a Mustang in the driveway that Bobby and I both paused briefly to examine. Driving was still four years in the future—a relative eternity at our age—but we had already begun to admire cars, to speculate about the masculine pickup trucks and muscle cars that we might drive at some unspecified point in the future.

The house was adorned with a few tasteful Halloween decorations: a tiny light bulb glowed inside a plastic jack-o'-lantern on the front porch. A white bed sheet, roughly manipulated to resemble a ghost, had been strung up in one of the shrubs.

"Do you know the people who live here?" Leah asked me. There would have been no point in asking Bobby, as he did not live in Shayton Estates.

"I don't know any of the families in this end of the neighborhood," I said.

And that made me think: What the heck had Matt Stefano been doing in Shayton Estates to begin with? Surely he didn't live here. Had he come here tonight with the express purpose of tracking me?

Pushing these thoughts aside, I pressed the doorbell.

The voice inside the house caused chills to ripple up my spine. It was a deep, booming voice:

"Open the door! Open the door!" it shouted.

Curiously, the voice also had an echo, as if the distinctly male presence were calling from the bottom of a ravine.

"That must be a recording," Bobby said.

"I don't think it's a recording," I said. The words had come as an immediate response to my ringing the doorbell.

"Well, then it's some kind of a sound effect."

Have it your way, Bobby, I thought. How could it be a "sound effect"? This wasn't a Hollywood studio, after all. This was a house in suburban Ohio. (And in 1980, stereo systems were pretty basic.)

Leah was about to offer her two cents, but then the door opened.

The woman before us appeared to be perfectly normal—at first glance. She might have been in her early- to mid-thirties. She was wearing what might be described as a "sexy witch" outfit: a sleeveless black gown that featured a short (though not indecently short) skirt, and a plunging neckline. Her light brown hair overflowed from beneath a store-bought witch's hat. Somewhat incongruously, she also wore glasses. They were encased in large, round plastic frames—the kind that were so popular in those days.

"Hello, children!" she said sweetly.

Once again, we heard the voice from somewhere deep in the house: *"Open the door!"*

The words seemed to vibrate through the front doorframe of the house.

The woman turned away from us to call back at the unseen source: *"I've got the door. You can stop now!"*

When she turned back to us, she quickly recovered from what might have been a look of annoyance. She was clearly unafraid of the man who had called out in that preternaturally low and rumbling pitch. This was some sort of an elaborate Halloween ruse —or something unusual was taking place here. I hadn't yet decided.

Was the woman's skin unusually pale? A part of me thought so; but it was difficult to say for sure in the dim lighting.

"Candy," she said, as if declaring her own absentmindedness. "That's what you children want: candy."

I know, even now, that all of us were feeling vaguely insulted at being referred to as children. None of us protested, though. We were the ones trick-or-treating, after all.

The woman stepped briefly away from the doorway and retrieved a serving bowl filled with "fun-size" chocolate bars and lollipops. Nothing out of order here, I thought.

When she gave me my Baby Ruth chocolate bar, the woman also favored me with a wide, friendly smile. Her mouth opened just wide enough for me to see her canine incisors.

They're fake, I thought. *They have to be.*

She pivoted to drop candy into the bags held by Leah and Bobby. I noticed that her hand brushed Bobby's. I saw Bobby stare back at the woman with wide-eyed amazement, then repulsion and fear. The woman shot a smile back at him. It might have been a private joke passed between the two of them. But Bobby turned away quickly, barely murmuring his thanks.

I stole a glance inside the house, which looked mostly normal, except for some atmospheric Halloween lighting. (This, of course, was nothing out of the ordinary.) My attention was drawn to something small and black that was walking jerkily past the woman's feet in the foyer.

The black cat walked like a robot, with stiff joints. The cat was no robot, though. Its black fur was genuine—and matted with blood.

"Hit by a car," the woman said in response to my unstated question.

Leah saw the cat, too, now, and she gasped aloud.

The woman stooped to pet the animal. It tilted its head back in response to her caress, but not like a normal cat would. Like its walking motions, the head movement was stiff and unnatural.

Rigor mortis, I thought, involuntarily.

"Hit by a car," the woman explained. As she scratched the animal's blood-caked pelt, she gave me another smile, another flash of those incisors. "You can revive them afterward, if you know what you're doing, but they're never the same."

Leah stammered on a reply, then turned and walked after Bobby.

The woman stood erect and allowed me to look at her in her full height, in that tight-fitting witch's outfit. I was an adolescent boy. My feelings about girls—women—were still brand-new, raw, and beyond my abilities to fully comprehend, let alone master. The frank invitation conveyed in her dress and pose both disturbed and stimulated me on multiple levels.

"Would you like to come in for a while?" she asked. "Your friends are leaving."

For a brief instant, my feelings of alarm and bashfulness dissipated. In their place came a sense that yes, stepping through that doorway would be the right thing to do. The strange woman and I could sit for a while. She would let me touch her—and she would touch me. She would give me a kiss with those incisors.

She tilted her head, and for the first time I caught a full glimpse of her eyes. The irises gleamed yellow. Some years would pass before I would realize that the irises of a wolf's eyes are also yellow; but I immediately grasped that something was very wrong here—and it would be dangerous for me to stay any longer.

"Jeff, come on!" Leah said from the end of the driveway.

Leah's voice—and the image of her in my mind—snapped me out of it. I turned my back on the woman without another word. I didn't bother to walk laterally across the walkway between the porch and the driveway. I stepped directly into the lawn, and beat a hasty retreat down to the road, where Bobby and Leah were anxiously waiting for me.

I heard the front door of the house close. I did not look back.

"Did you see that cat?" Leah asked me.

I nodded. I had seen the cat—and much, much more.

I wasn't quite up to talking about the woman's eyes just yet, nor even her teeth. My intuition told me that I had just made a slim escape from something—though I did not yet dare to name it. Not until I was a safe distance away from that house.

My vision began to spin now, and a wave of nausea surged through me. I separated myself from my friends and walked over to the nearest drainage ditch. I did not want to vomit in front of Leah, if I could help it.

"You all right, Jeff?" Leah asked.

I leaned over and braced my hands on my knees. The feeling of intense nausea passed. I was still shaking, but I rejoined my friends on the road.

"All right," Leah said, without slowing her pace. We were walking right by houses where we might have stopped for candy, but none of us seemed to care. "We need to talk about this."

"Okay, let's talk," Bobby said. "What exactly did we see back there?"

"Maybe nothing," Leah suggested weakly. Was she simply playing devil's advocate? I recalled how the brief and horrific transformation of the ghost boy had so upset her.

"It wasn't nothing," I said.

"Maybe not," Bobby allowed.

"Bobby," I said. "When that woman touched your hand, you made a face like you'd just seen a ghost. Then you practically ran away."

He stopped in the middle of the road. I noticed then that we were the only kids out on the street, even though this was a suburb, and it was still the first hour of trick-or-treat. Other kids should have been here. Where had they gone?

"Her hands were cold," Bobby began, in a hoarse whisper. "And her skin was—*what's that word*—clammy. Like she'd been swimming in ice water."

"Did you see her teeth?" I asked. "Or her eyes?"

"Wait a minute," Leah interjected. She did not volunteer whether she had glimpsed the woman's strange features or not, but her subsequent question strongly suggested that she had seen *something*. "So what are we saying here? Are we saying that woman was a *vampire*?"

Now that Leah had actually uttered the word (the same word that all of us were undoubtedly thinking) it sounded absurd. Yeah, *right* —vampires.

And yet, it *didn't* sound so absurd—not after everything we had seen, and in Bobby's case, felt. I had felt something, too, for that matter.

Without saying anything more to my friends for the moment, I began to assemble the rudiments of an explanation: The woman might have been a recently turned vampire. She was still presentable, still capable of interacting with the living. The man who had called out to her might have been a stronger vampire, one whose manner-isms and appearance had so changed that he was no longer presentable.

And that cat: Didn't witches and vampires supposedly maintain animal "familiars"? Something had obviously happened to that cat —*the woman had said that it had been hit by a car.*

She had also said something about "reviving" it.

"No way," Bobby said, dismissing Leah's suggestion of vampires in Withamsville. "She was putting us on."

"Sure," I countered. "And what about her teeth? Did you see her teeth? Did *either of you* see her teeth?"

"You can buy fake vampire teeth at the mall, or from those mail order ads on the back of comic books," Bobby answered. It was the same as it had been a few days ago, with the ghost boy. Already Bobby was beginning the process of rationalization, of making the evidence fit a comfortable reality. I figured that Leah would be on the same side. Nevertheless, I had seen what I had seen, and I wasn't backing down.

"She didn't buy those teeth from a comic book. And what about her skin? You were the one who felt her skin, and it freaked you out so bad you left the porch."

"Hey, it was a good trick, I'll admit." Bobby's tone was a bit testy. He didn't like my suggestion—however indirect—that he had been the first one to be scared, the first one of us to look away.

"Do you really believe that it was a 'trick'?"

"She could have been emptying ice trays in the kitchen."

I looked at Leah. She shrugged and looked away.

"How about this house?" She said. I think we were all eager to change the subject. This next house was two or three houses down from the home of the woman who might (and might not) have been a vampire.

The house was somewhat unkempt. It looked like the owner had missed the last mowing of the season. In the space between the front sidewalk and the exterior wall of the house, weeds competed for space with some scraggly-looking shrubbery that might have been rose bushes. It was the end of October, though, and their blooms were long gone, despite the relatively moderate weather.

We walked up the driveway, Leah leading the way. I watched the back of her head longingly. I wished, once again, that it had been only the two of us tonight. I didn't know exactly what I might have said to her, but I wasn't going to say anything of consequence with Bobby along as a third wheel.

Or was *I* the third wheel? Was Bobby the one that Leah really liked—or someone else, maybe? Trivial though the question may have been, it seemed to be a matter of life and death for me at the moment.

Distracted as I was by these thoughts, I didn't even notice the car that was parked in the driveway. But I would notice it shortly.

Leah—or it might have been Bobby—rang the doorbell.

We waited. There was no answer. However, there were clearly people inside. Not only could we see lights behind the shuttered and curtained windows along the front of the house, we could also hear music and voices coming from inside.

"Sounds like they're having a Halloween party," Leah said. "Should we go?"

"No," Bobby replied. "If they're having a Halloween party, then maybe they've got some good stuff inside."

Another half-minute passed and there was no answer. I was about to suggest that we leave; there were plenty of other houses. But then Bobby rang the doorbell again, and gave the door an insistent knock. We were committed now.

We heard the doorknob turn and the lock rotate in the tumbler. The front door swung open with a creak.

It was the ghost boy. He was clad in his usual attire: army surplus jacket, tee shirt, and jeans. *(Was there something wrong with his neck, though?)*

The ghost boy was completely unsurprised by our presence there. He might have been waiting for us to show up. In retrospect, he almost certainly was.

"Hey! Why don't you guys come in and join the party?" he beckoned. With a sweep of one arm he made as if to invite us in.

There was indeed a gathering taking place inside the house, as could have been surmised from the noise—even when the door had been closed. The interior of the house was bathed in a dull orange-red light that prevented me from discerning many details about the figures milling around inside.

I wasn't quite sure if Leah and Bobby even recognized him. Then Leah gasped.

I nearly gasped, too. There was definitely something wrong with the ghost boy's neck. On the left side, near the larynx, a huge portion of skin was rotted away. It wasn't a wound, mind you—it was decay.

"Come on in," he repeated, in a tone that was both deeper and rougher this time.

My attention was distracted as something rolled by: It was a wheelchair: The old man from the parking lot of the Village Market leered at me as he pushed his way horizontally past us on the other side of the ghost boy. Then he was gone from our field of vision.

Bobby had been silent until this point.

"Bullshit!" he said. "This is all a big put-on."

Then the ghost boy's guests began to emerge from the far corners of the house. In the kitchen, an adolescent boy with deathly pale skin limped toward us. I recognized him from the picture that had been printed in the local newspaper: He was Michael J. Hollis—the boy who had been struck and killed in traffic several summers ago, the boy whose grave marker had been placed in the front yard of a nearby house especially for Halloween night.

There were others in there as well: I saw Diane Wallace, walking with her head at an unnatural angle, a result of the accident that had killed her. James Platt was back there, too, and others as well.

I don't know exactly how many of them there were, but the house seemed suddenly to be full of them.

The ghost boy repeated his invitation. "Don't you want to come in? This is where all the cool kids hang out." He placed extraordinary emphasis on the word 'cool'. Everyone inside that house was cool— or rather, cold.

None of us needed to see any more. In a pell-mell fashion, like the children that we had only recently been, Bobby, Leah, and I fled.

As I ran toward the street, I caught a glance at the car parked in the driveway: It was a maroon Oldsmobile—a Cutlass sedan from the early 1960s.

"For twelve hours you will know no peace. For twelve hours you will be tested. And you're weak. You won't survive."

I repeated these words for my friends. They were the same words that the ghost boy had spoken to me, in the form of a malediction, on that afternoon I walked home alone.

Leah, Bobby, and I were standing in the middle of the street now. Before stopping, we had placed a comfortable distance between ourselves and the house where the ghost boy had been (and for that matter, the house of the strange woman who might have been a vampire, as well as the house with the lawn containing the uncannily realistic grave markers).

"So what are you saying, Jeff?" Bobby asked after I had given them an exhaustive account of my exchange with the ghost boy. "Are you saying that kid put some kind of a curse on you, and that now it's our curse, too, because we're with you tonight?"

I paused before answering. What Bobby was saying was essentially my interpretation of the situation, his obvious skepticism notwithstanding.

For some reason, the unusual happenings of the recent days had made my friends not only jittery, but touchy as well. This would cloud their judgment, I knew. And the divisions between the three of us might widen.

I was already scared, and I had reason to believe that the "curse" as Bobby called it, might be seriously dangerous as well as unnerving. So far, it had all been little more than a display of strange sights and sounds. But given the horrific nature of those sights and sounds, that was bound to change.

"I guess that 'curse' is as good a name for it as any," I replied. Do you have a better word?"

Bobby didn't answer me. He looked away. And for the first time ever, I saw real fear in Bobby Nagel's expression. Oh, sure—he was brave enough when facing down bullies of the St. Patrick's or even the Youngman variety. But he was at a loss here; there was nothing in his experience, or in his image of himself as a slightly-tougher-than-average seventh grader that told him how to handle this.

"This is not happening," Leah whispered. She looked away from me, too. "This is *not* happening."

Was it my imagination, or were my two friends showing signs of a mental breakdown?

This was an odd question to be asking, of course: I had by now more or less accepted that all this strange phenomena had to have at least some basis in reality.

It was easier to believe in ghosts than to fundamentally doubt my two friends—to seriously question their sanity. Like my parents and the comfortable home in which I'd thus far grown up, they had been with me for as long as I could remember.

Then a realization came to me: If we were going to find our way out of this, then I would have to take the lead. Although we were a pretty egalitarian threesome, I had always allowed Bobby to lead, on those rare occasions when a leader was needed.

But now Bobby was faltering. It was up to me. This frightened me as much as it gave me a surge of confidence.

I surveyed our surroundings: They were more or less normal, and now I could even see a few other trick-or-treaters, though they were far down the street and few in number. The latter was little reassurance, of course. Matt Stefano might be among them. More dead kids might be among them.

10

"We'll just double back," I said. "We'll go home."

"It's still early," Bobby objected.

"Are you going to tell me that you haven't had enough trick-or-treating for tonight?" I asked. "Let's face it: We were probably a little too old for this, anyway. We only went out tonight for the sake of 'one last time.'"

"For nostalgia's sake," Leah added.

"Yeah," I agreed. "That's as good a name for it as any, I suppose. I think we've all made enough memories for one night, and collected enough candy, too."

"I'll say," Leah said. "I don't care if I never taste chocolate again. I only want to get out of here. I just want this to stop."

"So what's your plan, Schaeffer?" Bobby relented. "Do you want to go back and drive a stake through the heart of that vampire lady? Maybe sprinkle holy water from church on the ghost boy and..." he involuntarily swallowed—"all those ghost kids?"

"No." I did have a plan in mind, but it didn't involve direct confrontation. "We should simply backtrack—go home. We can take a shortcut down Old Orchard Lane. That will take us within a quarter mile of Leah's house. You and I will walk Leah home. Then we'll go to my house. I'll get my mom or dad to drive you home."

This last step would be necessary because Bobby lived outside the neighborhood. I hadn't yet decided how much I was going to tell my parents about what had happened. Worst case, Bobby could plead stomach cramps or a twisted ankle. In any event, either Mom or Dad would probably agree.

Bobby nodded. "Okay."

"Leah?"

"Sure. That sounds like a good idea, Jeff. Simple and straight-forward."

"Let's go, then."

On the way back, we gave the house of the ghost boy a wide berth. Nevertheless, I saw Leah glance anxiously toward the doorway where the ghost boy and his unearthly guests had revealed themselves to us a scant ten minutes ago.

Taking a chance, I reached out and took her hand. She glanced at me in surprise at first, then relaxed and squeezed my hand back.

Despite the circumstances, warmth flooded through me—and another feeling that would become more familiar to me in the years immediately ahead. Puberty was new to me, and I was a bundle of raw nerve endings and unrestrained reactions.

Then I saw Bobby notice Leah and I holding hands. He looked away without comment.

I released Leah's hand when we passed the house of the grave markers. There were noises up ahead, and they didn't belong to people, in all likelihood. Maybe not even to ghosts.

"Is that a dog up there?" Bobby speculated.

There were a few vicious dogs in the neighborhood—or dogs that you were best to watch out for and avoid at the very least. Most of the year, they weren't an issue for us; but an overly aggressive dog was always a potential hazard for a kid on a bike. On more than one occasion during the previous summer, Bobby and I had pedaled madly away from a large German Shepherd or Doberman mix that had materialized from the perimeter of a neighborhood house and run barking down to the road.

We all stopped to listen to the growling in the distance. It didn't sound exactly like a dog, though. Whatever was making that noise had a bigger set of lungs than the average dog. There was also something about that growl that sounded distinctly unhealthy—as if the animal were having trouble breathing.

"That's not a dog," I said.

A large shape revealed itself by moving across several sets of porch lights. Although my instincts urged me to recoil (to run in the opposite direction, in fact) I forced myself to step forward by several paces, so that I could gain a better look.

Silhouetted against the moonlight, the oblong snout of a large bear revealed itself.

Bears, of course, are practically unknown in the populated regions of Ohio; and the bears that do exist in the Buckeye State are smaller black bears. The specimen far ahead of us must have been a full-grown grizzly. There are no wild grizzly bears east of the Mississippi, or far south of the Canadian border.

Some of these specifics would have been beyond my grasp on that night, but no one had to tell me that the bear's presence was unnatural.

Nor was the bear itself a normal phenomenon of nature. The animal ambulated with creaky, jerky movements. After pacing back and forth across the road several times, it stood in the middle of the blacktop pavement and barred our path.

"Oh, my," Leah said. "That—that thing is from the Dolbys' living room. Don't you recognize it, Jeff?"

It took me a moment to grasp what Leah was talking about. At the far end of our street lived an elderly couple, a Mr. and Mrs. Dolby. Despite the age difference, the Dolbys were well-loved among the neighborhood children. When I'd had a paper route two summers ago, Mr. Dolby had routinely tipped me extra when I came around for collections. The Dolbys were always good for the purchase of a raffle ticket to support little league, or a one-year magazine subscription to support the school band.

On one especially hot day, Mrs. Dolby had invited me to step inside their house while she retrieved my paper money (plus a glass of lemonade). That was when I'd noticed Mr. Dolby's bearskin rug.

"Oh, that old thing," Mrs. Dolby had explained. "That belonged to Mr. Dolby's grandfather. I believe that his grandfather's father shot the bear in Montana. That would have been sometime during the 1800s—not long after the Civil War, in fact."

"I've seen the rug," Leah explained now. "The bearskin rug. I remember it from a few years ago, back when I was still in Girl Scouts and we were selling cookies."

That explained the bear's almost mechanical movements. It was really a bear—a bear that had been dead for a very long time.

I recalled my mother mentioning something a week or so ago—about the Dolbys leaving early for Florida this year. So at least the reanimated bear carcass—if that was indeed what it was—wouldn't harm them. But our safety was another matter.

"We can't go that way," I said.

"Maybe we can go around it," Bobby suggested. Bobby separated himself from us and stepped into the grass of the adjacent lawn. He took a few steps forward, in the direction of our intended destination.

The bear moved laterally to counter him. It bellowed—a hollow, unnatural sound, nothing like a real bear, in all probability. But the message was clear: If we tried to go directly home, we would have to contend with that thing first.

Bobby walked carefully backward, his gaze fixed on the bear.

"I wonder if those jaws work?" he asked.

"Do you want to find out?" Leah challenged him.

The bear now moved two or three feet in our direction. It wasn't quite a charge, but it was enough to make us move correspondingly in the opposite direction—back the way we had been going.

"We can't go this way," I said. "We have to go back." I understood now what was happening—or at least I thought that I did. The bear was there for a purpose. We were not *supposed* to go home early—it wasn't going to be that easy.

The bear reared up on its hind legs. From this distance and angle, and given the poor lighting, it was impossible to discern if the bear was merely the hollow shell of the rug that it had been, or if it had taken on a more solid, substantial form.

In either case, though, the bear had those teeth—and I didn't doubt that the reanimated creature was dangerous.

"Where is 'back'?" Leah asked. "I thought we were already going back."

"I mean 'back' as in the way that we would have gone if none of this had happened," I explained. "We need to take the same route that we've taken every year. We need to complete our normal circuit of the neighborhood."

The bear let out a hollow, wheezing growl. A sudden stiff breeze caused a part of the rug to ripple audibly. Then we all heard the jaws move open and snap shut. Any questions about the danger posed by the teeth were thereby put to rest.

I began walking backward—in the direction whence we had come. Leah and Bobby both followed without any specific instructions from me.

"Are you sure about this, Schaeffer?" Bobby asked.

"I'm sure that we can't get past that bear," I said. "And I'm pretty sure that if we keep moving, we'll eventually get to the end of this."

"Of the 'curse'?"

"Like I asked you before: Do you have a better word for it?"

Bobby didn't reply. They both followed me, back past the house of the gravestones, and past the house where the ghost boy presumably still convened with his macabre guests.

I was the leader now. I was responsible for telling others what needed to be done—for the first time in my life.

I wasn't a formal leader, of course. No one had appointed me, nor had there been an election. I had become the leader by default. For a while, anyway, Bobby and Leah would do what I told them to do, and it was my de facto responsibility to guide them through this.

I had never led people before—I had never thought of myself as a leader in any way. I wondered if I was ready.

W e had walked perhaps an eighth of a mile when we heard the voices, and the sucking sounds.

It sounded like someone was digging holes in the muck of the surrounding front yards. In and of itself, that was not a particularly terrifying sound, but it had no logical explanation.

The voices were another matter. They were approximately human, but their words were as yet indistinguishable.

They were groaning—at us.

"Help me!" I heard one of the voices cry out. Then another plea for rescue. But rescue from what?

The three of us paused in the middle of the street.

"Look," Leah said. "Look around us."

The formerly grassy spaces of the surrounding yards were churning—with mud, and with human bodies that were struggling to reach the surface. We could see hands, torsos, and faces that were still mostly caked with mud.

Just a few paces from us, the body of an elderly woman broke through the mud. She was wearing a formal dress—the kind of dress that she might have been buried in—and half the skin on her face was gone. Her fingers, grasping toward us in the night air, were skeletal.

"Help me!" she pleaded.

"What the hell?" Bobby cried out.

I understood, as I had been the one to intuitively understand so much of what had happened over the past several days. These were the restless dead who were coming back for the night. The dead who were not content to move on, the dead who still craved life and the living.

As more of the bodies worked their way free, we could see that most of them were adults—presumably older adults. (*It was impossible to discern the death ages of many of them, rotted as they were.*) But there were also some children among them—youths our age and younger, who had been prematurely culled from the ranks of the living. They were especially insistent in their pleas to us.

So far, none of these undead had managed to pull or push completely free of the earth that bound them. They did not seem to threaten us in the same way that the bear did (and as other entities would, before the night was over), but there was something about their insistence that might have overwhelmed us.

At the age of twelve, I was only just beginning to understand the nature of my life force, how the desire to live, interact, take, and give impelled me. I was at the beginning of that journey, and these wretched creatures clawing their way through the mud had long since ended it.

They weren't evil, but they were jealous of us; they would have to be. They had once been like us, and look at them now.

If they managed to break free and reach us, what would they do? Would they let us escape easily?

Bobby and Leah both stood speechless and transfixed by the writhing bodies and their unanswerable, groaning pleas.

I dropped my bag of candy in the street, absently noticing that Bobby and Leah had also dropped theirs. I grabbed both of them by an arm nearest me.

"Come on," I said. "We have to get out of here."

Once again, Bobby and Leah did as I directed them. It did not take us long to move past the yards filled with corpses. They comprised no more than two or three lots on either side of us.

"What was that?" Bobby asked, shaking his head in disbelief. Bobby still couldn't force himself to believe all of this. The evidence, however, was now far too compelling for him to seriously propose that it was all some sort of an orchestrated hoax, or our collective delusion.

"We'll talk about it later," I said (though as I now recall, we never actually did). The cries of the grasping dead could still be faintly heard behind us, and their plaintive demands for help—for a share of the living force that each of us carried inside—had unnerved me. I wasn't ready to talk about this with others yet. I was still processing it.

But I wouldn't have much time to think. The houses and yards surrounding us were looking normal again. The national election being only days away, evidence of the contest was all around us. Even Halloween could not drown out politics. To the right of us, a green sign declared: "Reelect Carter and Mondale: A tested and trustworthy team." On the other side of the road, a competing sign exhorted: "Ronald Reagan for President: Let's make America great again." I wondered, vaguely, as a distraction from my fear and my weightier thoughts, if these two across-the-street neighbors maintained friendly relations despite their political differences.

These ruminations were interrupted by the utterance of my name, and an all-too-familiar curse word.

"Jeff Schaeffer, you pussy. There you are."

I looked around to see Matt Stefano standing in the middle of the road with two of his friends—Steve Wilmert and Tony Sparks. I was briefly back in the "normal world" now, and I might have been glad of that. Except that my version of the normal world was also inhabited by Matt Stefano and his friends.

Matt, Steve, and Tony had made no concessions to the holiday. They were not wearing costumes, and they were carrying no bags for gathering candy. They were clad in their usual afterschool outfits: faded and frayed blue jeans, denim jackets, and tee shirts.

I noticed a bulge in the breast pocket of Matt's jacket: The switch-blade, no doubt. Of course: I had seen him take it out only a short while ago.

The three of them assessed the three of us with expressions of open disdain, exchanging sneers with each other.

"What are you and Nagel supposed to be," Matt asked me, "a couple of faggot pirates?"

I considered letting the comment pass. There was really no fitting response. And we probably did look ridiculous, decked out as we were.

But Leah was there. Two things about tonight: I had already been through a lot (though, unbeknownst to me, much still lay ahead of me), and I had made some real progress with Leah. She had held my hand, after all.

And I wasn't going to allow Matt to ruin that—whatever the consequences.

"Just let us pass, Matt," I said. "We aren't bothering you."

"'Just let us pass!'" Matt mimicked in a falsetto. This prompted the expected laughs from both Steve and Tony.

Matt took several steps closer to us—closer to me, in particular. I was now distinctly conscious of the five or six inches of Matt's height advantage. He was nearly a full head taller than me. I didn't want to even speculate on his weight advantage—probably thirty pounds, at least.

"Tell me, Schaeffer," Matt said slowly. "What if I decide that I don't want to let you pass, huh? What's your plan then? You going to hide behind Nagel? Or maybe your girlfriend here?"

Matt's last remark caused an anger to flare within me. I did want Leah to be my girlfriend, of course. But strictly speaking, she wasn't yet, and Matt's sarcastic preemption of the idea might dash everything.

"It doesn't look like you came alone, either, Stefano," Bobby observed.

"Okay, then," Matt allowed, nodding. "How about it, Schaeffer?

Just you and me—man to man. Are you up to that? Or are you too much of a pussy?"

Stefano had placed me in the ultimate catch-22. A fight between Matt Stefano and me would be grossly unfair: He had numerous and decisive advantages in size, age, and experience. I had been in only a few fisticuffs in my entire life, and they had been childhood affairs—scuffles on the playground in the fourth or fifth grade. Matt Stefano, based on his age, should have been a high school kid. And he would fight like a high school kid.

On the other hand, I could not back down without admitting that I was afraid of him—which I was, despite my flashes of bravery and leadership tonight.

"Don't do it," Bobby said to me, in a sotto voce whisper. "You don't have to fight him. And the truth is—you can't win that fight."

"Shut up, Nagel!" Stefano said. Matt was about to shove Bobby when we all became aware of another presence on the street.

It was the ghost boy. He had interposed himself between Matt and his two friends. I can't say that I was glad to see him—not after seeing evidence of his true nature. But I was at least somewhat grateful for the distraction.

"Who are you?" Matt challenged, whirling on the ghost boy.

I thought: *Matt thinks he's a normal kid.* I expected Matt to resort to his tough guy routine. Then the ghost boy would turn into something horrible, and Matt would run shrieking away. Maybe the ghost boy would do even worse to Matt. At that moment, I wouldn't have objected.

That wasn't what happened, though. The ghost boy began talking to Matt and his two accomplices, in a low murmuring voice that was almost inaudible from where Leah, Bobby, and I stood. I saw Matt's posture relax. Tony and Steve relaxed, too.

The ghost boy stopped talking and pointed to an unseen location behind us. Matt and his two friends suddenly broke ranks, and all three of them walked around and past us. Leah, Bobby, and I might have been trees or fence posts.

I briefly looked over my shoulder to watch them go. They didn't even glance back at us. They were gone. We had escaped—or maybe we had been saved.

The three older boys had walked in the direction of the groaning, pleading undead. I wondered if they would encounter the apparitions, too. Then I decided that no, they probably would not. Matt, Tony, and Steve were not among my companions, so they would be unaffected by the curse.

The ghost boy stared directly at me and said: "Don't be thinking that I saved you. He might take you another night—if you live that long. But tonight you're ours. If you live through tonight, he can have you, for all I care."

The ghost boy turned away and walked into one of the adjacent yards. We all saw what happened next: When he passed by the trunk of a large tree, his body dissolved into a smoky ether; then that was gone, too.

Leah sighed aloud, shaking her head in disbelief at all that she had just experienced. Her body was quivering, even though it wasn't all that cold yet. I was going to say something, until I noted that Bobby and I were trembling too—a delayed reaction, I supposed.

Leah looked to Bobby, and then to me. "What the—" she began.

"Later," I said. "We'll talk about it later. Right now, we need to keep walking."

And so we did.

E ven from a distance, something seemed unnatural about the girl who was sitting in the tree swing.

First of all, there was the situation itself: Here it was, Halloween night; and although this section of the neighborhood was without trick-or-treaters, we knew that it must still be within the scheduled hours for the activity. Despite all that had happened, we had not been gone for much longer than an hour, we estimated.

Why would the girl be sitting in a tree swing in someone's front yard on Halloween night?

And then there was the dress: Girls hadn't worn dresses like that since before my grandparents were born. No—scratch that—since before my grandparents' grandparents were born. It was a dress not from any point in the twentieth century, but from much earlier.

The tree swing hung from the branch of a large tree in the middle of someone's front yard. The house was a simple one-story ranch house. We were in the older part of the neighborhood now, on one of the streets that conjoined with Shayton Estates. The houses on this street dated back to the immediate postwar era, when builders throughout the country had scrambled to provide housing for all those returning GIs.

But this girl would have looked out-of-place even in that era. Her white dress extended nearly to her ankles and it billowed at the bottom. This was a dress from back in the days when women wore full-length undergarments.

As we approached, she continued to swing in the dark, her hands gripping the swing's thick ropes, her long dark hair cascading down her back.

Her skin was pale. And it might have been my imagination, but it was faintly glowing in the moonlight.

We stopped in front of the house. The girl was a sight to behold. It wouldn't do to simply walk by her without comment.

"Don't talk to her," Bobby said. "She's a ghost."

I was struck by Bobby's attitudinal shift. An hour ago, Bobby had been ready to deny the existence of any ghosts, and now he had been the first to identify this one.

"If she's a ghost," Leah said, "then she doesn't seem to be a bad one. Look at her—she's about our age, more or less."

This much was true: I would have placed the girl's age at twelve or thirteen years old—fourteen at the maximum. But the relevant question was: How long had she been twelve to fourteen? Depending on the answer, she could be very, very old indeed by another standard of measurement.

"We should talk to her," Leah said.

"Why?" Bobby protested. "Why do we have to talk to her? Why can't we keep moving, and then we'll get to the end of all this?"

"Maybe we shouldn't," I said. Thus far, talking to supernatural entities hadn't yielded the best results.

"If you guys won't, then I will."

The girl then stopped swinging and turned around in the swing to stare at us.

"That isn't very nice of you," the girl said, "talking about me like I'm not even here."

I noticed that the girl was crying. But surely our talking about her couldn't have upset her so.

Throwing caution aside, Leah stepped off the blacktop and onto the grass of the front lawn. She leapt across the narrow drainage ditch and stood within lunging distance of the girl in the swing. *Lunging distance,* I thought. If this ghost was a bad one, then Leah could be taken, and we could do nothing to help her.

I looked at Bobby and shrugged. We didn't know yet if the girl was dangerous. In either case, I didn't intend to let Leah face her alone.

I followed Leah, stepping across the ditch and onto the lawn. Bobby followed me without further protest or comment.

"Why are you crying?" Leah asked the girl. "What's wrong?"

"I can't find my parents!" she said, with a loud sob.

"Where do your parents live?"

I let Leah ask her question, but it occurred to me that Leah had failed to make an important connection: This girl's parents probably didn't "live" anywhere anymore.

"They're supposed to live here!" she cried. "This is where my family's apple orchard is supposed to be."

I might have heard something once about the land around here having been an apple orchard a long time ago. There was evidence for this in some of the street names. The street we were walking down was Applegate Drive. And we had planned to take a shortcut through Old Orchard Lane—before our way was blocked by Mr. Dolby's bear.

But all that was a long, long time ago, if it had ever been at all. This was a memory that this girl—if she was indeed around our age —could not possibly possess.

Leah said: "You know, I heard something about this land being an apple orchard."

"I heard about it, too. But do you know how long ago that was?"

I wanted to get away from this girl on the swing, even though she did not appear to represent an immediate threat to us. If asked, I wouldn't have been able to put my objection into words at that time. Having thought about it over the years, I've since decided that there was simply something unnatural and vaguely indecent about the dead and the living mixing in this way.

The corpses writhing in the mud were still fresh in my memory, their desire for our life force naked and unrestrained. I've read in the intervening years that when spirits appear to the living, they never do so idly. A ghost always has an agenda, a desire. Spirits, when they appear to us, always want *something*.

But Leah seemed so fascinated with this girl. And as I've already told you, I was quite fascinated with Leah. That was what kept me there, even though my better judgment told me to move on.

"Don't cry," Leah encouraged the girl. "It can't be that bad. Maybe we—maybe we can help you."

As soon as Leah uttered those words, I desperately wished that she could have unsaid them.

"Really?" the girl stopped her sobbing. "Do you mean it?"

"Of course we mean it," Leah replied. "What's your name?"

"Elmira," she said. "And you?"

Leah introduced each of us. "My name is Leah, and these two are Bobby and Jeff."

The girl acknowledged us with a slight tilt of her head, though she didn't seem overly interested. As she inclined her head toward Bobby, I saw—or thought I saw—a momentary glimpse of a section of the house's brick wall behind her. The brickwork was briefly visible through the girl's body—or so it seemed.

And, of course, she would be named something old-fashioned like Elmira. She wouldn't be a Julie or a Jennifer or a Kim. I had never met anyone named Elmira. Nor have I since then, for the record.

"You know," Elmira said, brightening, "maybe I can help *you* first."

"How can you help us?" Bobby queried. I noticed that Bobby was deliberately maintaining a cautious distance from Elmira. He didn't trust her.

"Well," Elmira turned to stare at Bobby, and then at me. For a split second, her eyes were all black pupil. And then they were relatively normal again.

She's trying to appear to us in a certain way, I thought, *a way that she believes will make us more comfortable. But it's difficult for her; it takes effort.*

Yet the real question was: *What did she want from us?*

"The three of you shouldn't be here, should you?"

I was about to ask Elmira exactly what she meant by that, but I decided that there was nothing to be gained by playing games, by maintaining pretenses.

"No," I said. "We're here because something—someone—put a curse on me. And my friends are here because of me." I sighed. "Because they're with me."

"You will see things tonight," Elmira began, "as you continue on your journey."

"Big newsflash," Bobby said. "Like we haven't already!"

Leah shushed him.

"What you have to do," Elmira continued, "is keep moving. And eventually, you'll reach the end."

I was afraid of this girl, as I was afraid of so much we had seen tonight. But I also sensed that if she was offering her insights to us, they might be useful.

"Can anything out here," I asked tentatively, "can anything out here really hurt us?"

"Oh yes," she said, turning to me again—and again I saw a brief flash of solid black where the whites of her eyes should have been. "You must be very careful. You aren't—where you came from anymore, but you already know that, don't you?"

"What are you talking about?" Bobby pressed, clearly irritated now. "We're on Applegate Drive. Applegate Drive has been here since before any of us were born."

Elmira ignored Bobby, but she continued to stare at me. I understood what she was saying. I remembered what Mr. Snyder had said about Halloween being a "liminal" time. Perhaps the curse—if that was indeed what it was—had exploited the seasonally thin boundaries between our world and one of the unseen ones.

What Bobby was saying was correct—in a sense: We were on plain old Applegate Drive. And at the same time, we *weren't* on plain old Applegate Drive.

"Keep moving," she repeated. "If you do, you'll get to the end. Eventually."

"Well, thanks!" Bobby said, with the typical sarcasm of an

emotionally distraught seventh grader. "Thanks for that great advice. Anyway, we'll be off now."

Bobby started to leave, but Leah halted him.

"Wait," Leah said. "We have to do something for her." She took a deep breath. "If we can, that is."

Elmira gripped the thick ropes of the swing. I wondered what would happen if I grabbed one of those ropes—or tried to: Would my hand simply pass through it?

She began gently sobbing again. "I didn't know! I didn't know!"

"What didn't you know, Elmira?" Leah asked. "Please don't cry."

"I didn't know that the woods were full of Indians! It was supposed to be safe here."

She turned her head, and we now saw an aspect of her features that we hadn't seen before. Perhaps she had been consciously hiding it—suppressing its manifestation, or perhaps it had simply been hidden by the angle of her head.

On the other side of her head was a deep gash that penetrated hair, skin, and bone. It was a wide, deep, open wound. A fatal wound. Elmira's ear was missing on that side, and I could see a patch of white that must have been the upper portion of her jawbone.

Leah noticed and gasped.

"Oh, damn," Bobby said in a befuddled whisper. Despite Leah's earlier insistence to the contrary, he took several steps away from Elmira and her ruined head, back toward the blacktop of Applegate Drive.

"I'm sorry," Bobby said. "I'm sorry. I can't do this."

"I miss my parents!" Elmira shouted, pulling my attention away from Bobby. She was staring at me with an imploring frown—a look of desperation. "Can you help me find them?"

"How?" I asked. Her request didn't make sense. "How do you expect us to do that?"

"I just went for a little walk that day! I didn't go far from the house —not that far, anyway. And then I got to the edge of the clearing, and there were the Indians!"

I was starting to piece the puzzle together: Shayton Estates was, as the crow flies, less than ten miles from the Ohio River. In the early days of the American republic, this land had been part of the Ohio Country, and the land to the south of the river had been Kentucky—a hunting ground of the Shawnee.

For decades the land on both sides of the Ohio River had been contested by both whites and Native Americans. There had been plenty of atrocities committed by both sides. The land that now comprised southern Ohio and northern Kentucky had been soaked with blood, many times over.

Elmira was oblivious to my attempts to clarify matters, and Bobby had all but checked out of the entire situation. Leah was still actively engaged, though, despite her involuntary horror at one side of Elmira's head.

"There," Leah said. "She has to go through that gate."

I looked in the direction that Leah was pointing. It was the gate to the fenced-in back yard of this house, but it was something more, too.

I could see a vast, but extremely faint image like a desert mirage: a log cabin built in the sunlit clearing of the long-ago wilderness.

Elmira's parents would be there, I felt sure—and so did Leah. Whether she would find them in her current state, or as she had been in life, I would not have ventured a guess. That clearing in the woods might have been Elmira's version of "the light" that spirits are always supposed to head toward. Or it might have been a land as real and corporeal as our world of October 1980.

Maybe Elmira would find what we approximate by the term "heaven". Maybe she would have another chance at that long-lost life. I had no idea.

Elmira, though, seemed to know about the gate.

"I've tried to go there," she said. "But he won't let me."

"Who is 'he'?" I asked. I had a feeling that I was not going to like the answer.

"The tree," Elmira answered.

"The tree?" I now noticed the large tree that stood to the left of the gate. It looked completely ordinary to me. In this older section of the neighborhood, there were many old trees that predated even the postwar housing developments. There were pin oaks that might be seventy or eighty years old. The trees were one of the charms of the neighborhood, my mother often said.

"It's a very bad tree," Elmira explained.

I heard a creaking sound high overhead. From his new position at the edge of the front lawn, within leaping distance of the roadway, Bobby called out, "Oh, man—that tree just *moved!*"

For the time being, I had no choice but to take Bobby's word on the matter. My view was partially blocked by the nearby tree to which Elmira's swing was affixed, and some other, smaller maple trees clustered in the front yard. The big tree—the one Elmira called the "bad tree"—was a massive pin oak. Its trunk was thicker than a grown man's body, and it towered to a massive height, far above the ranch homes in this section of Applegate Drive.

"Was that the wind?" I asked hopefully.

Leah replied: "It wasn't the wind." And she was right. There wasn't the slightest breeze at the moment.

"Every time I try to go through the gate," Elmira said, "he stops me. He wants me to be stuck here forever. So I'll *never* find my parents!"

Incredible as this sounds—and incredible as it seems looking back on that night—the massive pin oak seemed to hear her. I heard a deep, bellowing laugh, cruel and malignant. The laugh was accompanied by the sounds of wood splintering, of small branches falling to the earth.

"Let me guess," I began. "I'll bet you want us to open that gate for you."

Elmira turned around in her swing, treating me to another look at her ruined head. *"You can do it,"* she declared desperately. *"People from the other side can do things that people from this side can't do."*

I heard another series of cracking, splintering sounds. There was a disturbance amid the branches of the harmless maple trees that were closer to me. The big pin oak was moving its branches around like arms, I surmised. That would figure, wouldn't it? The bad tree would be able to use its branches as weapons. It had appointed itself the guardian of the gate, and it had the means to enforce its will.

"*I'll* do it," Leah said, sensing my hesitation.

"No," I objected. "*I* will."

In truth I didn't want to, though. And in truth I was more than a little angry at Elmira. Yes, I felt sorry for her and all, but I also believed that she had lured us with false pretenses. She had known all along where her parents were—she hadn't needed our help with that. What she needed was our human bodies—mine, specifically. As a more substantial, corporeal presence, I could presumably race back there and fling open the gate.

If I wasn't killed in the process, that was.

Bobby said from the edge of the front yard: "I'm not kidding, Schaeffer, that thing is moving."

I had no doubt that Bobby was telling the truth. I could hear the evidence for myself overhead, in the crackling of the branches. I could feel it in the twigs that were raining down with each movement of the big pin oak.

And at the same time, I thought: How hard could it be? All I had to do was open the gate, right?

The answer: It could be plenty hard; it could be deadly.

There are times when you have to seize the initiative in an opportune moment of courage, before excessive contemplation of the circumstances forces you to change your mind.

Without further comment, I ran in the direction of the gate, and tried my utmost to ignore the sounds of the crackling branches, and the blood-chilling groans of the massive pin oak.

It wasn't a long run; my sprint carried me to the gate in a matter of seconds.

I stood before the gate, and the big oak tree. I could feel the earth beneath my feet vibrating now: The tree's roots were pulsating in the loam and clay underneath the lawn.

I knew it would be better to ignore the tree and focus only on the gate, but I couldn't resist. I gazed up at the trunk of the tree. About fifteen feet up, near the lowest of the oak's branches, I saw the impossible.

In the middle of the trunk, the gash of a large grimace proved for once and for all that this was no ordinary oak tree. I could see teeth inside that mouth—in the darkness they appeared to be the same color as the bark, but they were long and serrated.

I also saw two eyes—these were only slightly lighter than the bark, but clearly distinguishable. The eyes rolled downward to look at me.

Another reverberating, furious sound issued from deep within the trunk of the pin oak. The bark began to crack; the pin oak seemed to sense what I was about to do, and it wanted to stop me.

I turned away from the tree and began fiddling with the gate. Despite the significance of the gate for Elmira, despite her difficulty in reaching the gate, there was nothing about the gate itself that was particularly difficult. It was secured with a standard sliding latch; there was no padlock.

I released the latch and pulled the gate open. What I saw was not the late twentieth-century suburban backyard that should have been there —but a clearing in a long-gone woods, dominated by a humble log cabin. I was not drawn to either the clearing or the cabin. I knew, seemingly by instinct, that both represented a world that I was not rightfully a part of. I recoiled from the entire scene, in fact. But to Elmira this would be home. The world of the clearing represented what she had known and loved in life, before her unfortunate encounter with a roaming band of Shawnee warriors. The open gate, likewise, would provide her with a pathway out of her long exile—a pathway back home.

"Come *now!*" I shouted at her. The tree produced a sound that was a grating, hate-filled gurgle. I could hear more cracks as it swung its branches overhead. Ironically, my proximity to the trunk kept me safe from the branches; but there were many unanswered questions: Could the pin oak force its limbs to bend downwards? And even more terrifying—could the body of the trunk itself be compelled to move?

Elmira jumped down from her swing. She did not pause to bid

Leah farewell—an omission which, I think, disappointed the latter more than she would have admitted. I watched as Elmira covered the short distance between the swing and the gate, and tried to ignore the increasingly loud and threatening protests from the gate's guardian.

The ghost girl looked briefly at me as she passed through the gate. She mouthed something at me that I did not understand. I assumed that she was thanking me.

Once Elmira was cleanly through, both the girl and the clearing began to dissolve into a mist, and the mist blended into a more conventional scene: a wooded suburban back yard with an above-ground swimming pool. An aluminum shed painted white.

But the pin oak remained in its animated and violent state. Its eyes were fixed on me now, baleful and filled with a depth of hatred that I would not have previously imagined possible. The tree—or the dark spirit that inhabited the tree—wanted to tear my limbs off. It wanted to crush my body and grind it into mush.

"Jeff!" It was Leah. "Jeff! Get away from there. Hurry!"

I saw that Leah was looking up at some new development, and so I looked up, too. Against the moonlit sky, I could see several of the oak tree's huge branches gradually bending downward, as if long-dormant and stiffened joints were being exerted into action. The bending motion was slow, and it was accompanied by much cracking overhead; but it was happening.

I had been in this spot too long already, I suddenly realized. Without so much as another glance at the tree, the newly exposed back yard, or the open gate, I bolted back in the direction of my friends.

I was halfway to Leah when I heard a particularly sharp series of cracks and a loud whooshing sound.

"Jeff!" Leah screamed. *"Duck!"*

I did more than duck. I dove to the ground.

I felt rather than saw the branch pass over my head. I rolled over onto my back, and I saw the branch swing away from me. The limb was as thick as a telephone pole. The intention had been to knock me down with what would have been a fatal blow.

I righted myself and scrambled backward as the limb swung back in my direction. Now I got a look at how completely the huge branch had been transformed. At the end of the branch was not a simple endpoint, but three, long, multi-jointed fingers that formed a crude hand.

A hand that was easily four feet in height.

I jumped backward as the hand plunged crudely but swiftly in my direction. The trunk was out of sight now, and the tree was probably grasping blindly for me, directed by the vibrations of my feet on the earth.

The tips of the wooden fingers went past my face in a blur. They dug into the lawn, throwing up dirt and grass.

"Jeff, come on!" It was Leah again. I thought I heard Bobby call out my name, too.

I ran faster than I had ever run in my life—toward Leah and the harmless tree (where, I vaguely noticed, Elmira's swing no longer hung). When I was most of the way there, Leah abandoned her position and ran on ahead of me, back to where Bobby was waiting.

The three of us stood there at the edge of Applegate Drive for a while, watching in disbelief as several of the big oak tree's branches twisted about in the air. Then a branch would dip to the lawn, and the makeshift hand at the branch's tip would grope about for the intruder who was now safely out of range, throwing up dirt and the dry late autumn turf.

Eventually it stopped. The tree (or, as I now believe, the errant spirit that possessed the tree) finally understood that the contest was over, and that it had lost. Elmira was (we could only assume) now safely on the other side of the boundary. And I was forever beyond the tree's reach; I vowed that I would never again set foot on that particular lawn, even after all of this was over, even in the bright light of a warm June afternoon.

The pin oak was just an ordinary tree again. The bellowing from the center of the trunk had ceased. All of its bare branches were restored to their fixed, aloft positions; and though they cast somewhat sinister silhouettes against the moonlight, their hands had been retracted.

"Tell me that didn't just happen," Bobby said.

"It happened," Leah contradicted him. "It happened, all right."

Then Leah looked at me with an expression that I can still clearly remember—even now, as I plod through the long march of middle age.

She was staring at me with unmasked admiration. She had wanted the gate to be opened for Elmira. In her spontaneous attachment to the ghostly girl, that task had been so important to Leah.

And I had accomplished it.

Leah smiled at me, and not knowing what else to do, I simply smiled back.

"Thank you," she said, "for what you did back there."

I knew that I must have been blushing. For the first time all evening, I was actually grateful for the dark.

"You—you're welcome," I said, with an unsteadiness that belied the comparatively brave act that I had just accomplished.

"Well," Leah said. "This—whatever it was, seems to be over. Let's get going again, shall we?"

13

For a while after that Leah walked on ahead of us, and I walked alone with Bobby.

He had been unusually silent after the incident with Elmira and the tree, and I thought I knew what was bothering him. He was downcast, avoiding direct eye contact with me even as we walked along shoulder-to-shoulder.

Our plan was to continue walking down Applegate Drive, and then we would turn right onto a street called Farrow Lane. Farrow Lane would eventually lead us back home.

There was to be no more trick-or-treating, of course. The streets were practically empty, anyway. Every once in a while we would pass a cluster of trick-or-treaters. But I noticed a pattern: If I looked away from them for any length of time, I would find that they had vanished when I looked back at them.

Leah, Bobby, and I were walking through our neighborhood, and yet we were walking through someplace else, too. It was as if we were constantly shifting back and forth between two worlds.

"You beat me back there," Bobby said without malice. His tone suggested that I had just bested him at some childish game, like pick-up basketball or arm-wrestling.

"What are you talking about?" I asked. My question was somewhat disingenuous. I did know what Bobby was talking about; and yet I wanted to hear him explicitly affirm it. Leah was still walking a few paces ahead of us, but I wondered how much of our conversation she could overhear.

"You know darn well what I mean, Schaeffer. I panicked when that tree—became whatever the heck it was. To tell you the truth, I was even afraid of that freaky girl. I saw the other side of her head, and it scared me."

"She kind of scared me, too," I admitted.

"Yeah, but you didn't run away from her."

"You didn't run away from her, either."

"What you mean is that I ran away from the tree." He mock-punched my arm. "Okay, Schaeffer, I'll admit it: You looked pretty good back there. I know you were scared, too; but the point is that you didn't back down; you didn't run away. In fact, you walked over to that thing on purpose, and you opened that gate."

I shrugged. "I didn't really take the time to think about it," I said. I'm sure Bobby wasn't deceived by my faux modesty. I was going to assure him that this wasn't a contest, but neither one of us would have been fooled by that line, either.

There were two truths here, which I dared not name, and which Bobby was not anxious to name, either: First, it *was* a contest. When you are twelve years old, practically everything is a contest.

Secondly, I couldn't pretend that I had done what I had done out of any altruistic concern for Elmira. I was the same boy who had callously left my little sister at home that night, the same boy who saw no obligation to lessen my overworked father's burden by taking on some adult responsibilities.

I had opened that gate for *Leah*, or rather, in order to prove something to Leah about myself. I had wanted to show her that I was no longer the hapless Jeff Schaeffer who hid behind a façade of constant good humor, who was a helpless target for bullies like Matt Stefano and his friends.

So I had done the right thing—most people would say so. But I had done the right thing for selfish reasons.

If you do the right thing for selfish reasons, does that detract from the rightness of the act itself? I didn't know the answer, not for sure. And now—nearly thirty-five years after that night—I am still not sure.

"Leah," I said, calling out to her. "Be careful. Come back here with us."

Leah turned around and gave me a questioning raise of her eyebrows, but she followed my instructions. She walked back to stand with Bobby and me, who were now stopped in the middle of the road.

"What is it, Schaeffer?" Bobby asked.

"That house up there," I said. "That's 1371 Applegate Drive."

"So what?" Bobby replied.

"Oh," Leah said. "Now I understand. I know about that house." She shivered, and pushed her body against me in a chaste let's-keep-warm gesture. "It feels colder, all of a sudden, doesn't it? And—oh, look you guys—look at those windows!"

THE HOUSE at 1371 Applegate Drive was the closest thing that our neighborhood had to a haunted house, although no one—until that night, at least—had ever claimed to have actually seen a ghost there.

The house had been built a full generation before the houses that Leah and I lived in; and the house's tragedy had taken place nearly a decade before any of us had been born.

One night in the early winter of 1959, a man named Donald Shipley had come home from work one night and murdered his wife and two children before turning a gun on himself.

The "Shipley house" thereafter assumed its place in neighborhood folklore. But the Shipley house's precise identity in the local imagination was complex and subject to change. The Shipley house wasn't a lone, dilapidated Victorian standing on a hillside in a remote area. (Houses such as these often become magnets for urban legends based on their appearances alone—regardless of their history.) The

Shipley house was an ordinary-looking ranch house, built in a cookie-cutter fashion to resemble the houses all around it. Nothing about the house particularly stood out, unless you knew what had taken place there. It was easy to forget that the Shipley house was in any way different from any other tract home on Applegate Drive.

And people often did forget. When it was occupied, the macabre history of the Shipley house was more or less ignored. I didn't move in adult circles back then, of course; but I suspect that this was partly in deference to the occupants at any given time. No one wants to be reminded that they are paying the mortgage on a house where three murders and a suicide took place.

But when the house lay vacant (as was the case in October of 1980) it became the "Shipley House"—a proper noun, the house where Donald Shipley had come home one night, perhaps deranged, perhaps hearing voices, and committed his unspeakable acts. When the house lay vacant, people avoided walking by it after dark, and children held their breath and crossed their fingers as they passed by it on their bicycles.

No one was particularly surprised by the fact that the Shipley house stood unoccupied more often than the other houses in the neighborhood. The home was what real estate agents refer to as a *stigmatized property*. Such a home is usually sold at a steep discount, and is therefore not considered to be a sound investment.

From what I had been told, there was discussion at one point (way, way back, not long after the murders) of demolishing the house and building a new one on the lot. But (and again, all this is hearsay so far as I knew) the bank that held the deed on the Shipley house simply wanted to be rid of the property. So early in 1960, the house was offered for sale at a tempting discount, and it acquired new owners.

The problem was that the Shipley house frequently acquired new owners, and no set of owners ever seemed to stay in it for very long. To the best of my knowledge, none of these owners ever made explicit claims of experiencing paranormal activity. Whether they actually did or did not was a matter of speculation. Among children, ghost stories are gems that are eagerly collected and exchanged at sleepovers and over languorous discussions on long summer afternoons. Among adults, a preoccupation with the paranormal is regarded as a sign of daftness at best—of derangement at worst. So if any of the adult owners of the Shipley house ever had any trouble in that regard, they kept it to themselves. They also limited their stays in the Shipley house to no more than two or three years, it seemed.

I WAS THEREFORE NOT ESPECIALLY SURPRISED to see that the windows of the Shipley house glowed with an odd purplish light. As we drew closer, I could see exactly what Leah was talking about: All of the windows were covered with drapes and shutters; but the light behind them sent shifting shades of violet and amethyst radiating outward.

The Shipley house was active tonight—I suppose that we should have expected as much.

The house was presently vacant, after all. Whatever forces did hold sway there would be emboldened by the absence of the living. And needless to say, the unique presence that was terrorizing us tonight (the "curse" as the three of us had now generally taken to calling it), had exposed and awakened whatever spiritual entities ordinarily lied dormant around the neighborhood.

Consider Elmira, for example, and the malevolent presence in the pin oak tree that had been so intent on keeping her captive—or holding her back, at the very least. How many times had I passed by that house, riding my bike on summer days, or riding in the back seat of my parents' car? But I had been completely unaware that either Elmira or the pin oak tree had existed at all.

Likewise, the Shipley house had never assumed a prominent place in my imagination. I suppose I avoided the house by default— but no more than the other kids in the neighborhood did. It was simply my custom to pass by it quickly. Where reputedly haunted houses are concerned, there is no point in taking unnecessary chances.

But so far, this was not a night that would permit us to avoid much of anything. I therefore had to make a quick assessment of the Shipley house: Did it threaten us—or could we walk past it without being molested?

"We need to stay away from that house," I said. I grabbed both Leah and Bobby by the shoulder, clasping one friend with each hand.

"What's the big deal?" Bobby asked. "Other than the obvious fact that the windows are glowing? Damn—that is weird. 'Psychedelic', as my old man would say."

Bobby's father, in addition to being an absentee father, was a hippy after a certain fashion. From what I had gathered, though, he wasn't one of those docile hippies who sat around humming Buddhist sutras and preaching peace and love. He was more the kind of hippy who might have ridden with a motorcycle gang at some point, in addition to possibly becoming involved with the illegal gun and drug running that had proliferated during that turbulent decade.

But like everyone from the sixties, Bobby's father spoke the lingo. "Psychedelic" was the kind of word that would be at the tip of Bobby's father's tongue. And while there was indeed something "psychedelic" about those shifting, kaleidoscopic purple lights, it was important to remember that a strobe light wasn't generating them. Like so much else that had happened this night, those lights shouldn't be there. They *weren't* there, if you wanted to be technical about it; we were probably the only ones who could have seen them.

Bobby shrugged my hand away—not angrily, but insistently. I released Leah's shoulder, too.

"We have to be careful," I said. "We can't go in there."

"Who's talking about going inside?" Bobby asked. "But we've gotta walk by it, right? Otherwise we stand in this one spot all night."

Bobby took a step forward, and then all of us jumped at the sound of the loud caws.

In the middle of the driveway a flock of crows had gathered. I had not seen them descend from the sky; perhaps they had been there all along. The birds were assembled in what appeared to be a formation. The purple light from the windows gave them disproportionately long shadows.

The crows were watching us. The scene was doubly macabre. First of all, most crows want nothing to do with humans. But even more than that, crows are not typically nocturnal birds.

"Stupid birds!" Bobby shouted. He ran forward, and the crows finally scattered, accompanied by more furious caws and the beating of wings. They did not go far, though. The crows alighted on the roof of the Shipley house. They were less visible in their new position, but we could still see their outlines.

I knew that Bobby was using anger as a defense mechanism. He was built for conflicts of the straightforward, rough-and-tumble variety. Since our initial encounters with the ghost boy, he had found himself at a loss, unable to cope with these things that he did not understand.

His response had alternately been denial, anger, and even flight. (Neither of us had forgotten his failure to stand by me as I faced the oak tree.)

I begrudged him none of this, because I knew that he was still braver, still more capable than me in his own way. But I also feared that his peculiar weaknesses would become liabilities for all of us tonight.

As we had been warned, these phenomena were not mere illusions. They were dangerous; I had found that out when those branches had descended from the sky, when one large tree limb had nearly killed me with a single blow. Bobby was shouting and running about recklessly when he should have proceeded quietly and with caution. His bluster scared me almost as much as what might be watching us from inside the Shipley house.

Just then, the front door of the Shipley house creaked open.

The ancient creature standing in the doorway might best be described as a witch, though that would be only an approximation. She—it—was slightly less than six feet in height, barrel-chested and clad in black robes. Her long, grey hair fell in clumps from a pallid, wart-covered scalp. She had a long nose and a pointy chin, just like the stereotyped witches of Halloween artwork, who have lost all but the vaguest traces of their humanity.

"What is that?" Leah whispered to me. "I've heard all the stories of the Shipley house, but nothing—nothing that could explain her. Or it—or..." Leah's voice trailed off, her questioning thought incomplete.

I didn't answer Leah at that time, but I thought I had an inkling of an idea. The Shipley house, by its very nature, attracted wandering evil things. This creature—which I'll call a witch for lack of a more precise term—would have been drawn by the dark energies that were collected and distilled inside this house.

The witch watched us, looking at each of us slowly in turn.

Then her gaze settled on Bobby. The witch smiled, revealing a jaw full of long, serrated teeth.

She stepped back from the doorway, and I was on the verge of believing that despite our troubles thus far, we would bypass what was probably the most spiritually active location in the neighborhood with no significant problems.

Then Bobby, without providing any explanation whatsoever, suddenly began running—toward the still open door of the Shipley house.

14

I called out after Bobby, but he wasn't listening to me. He didn't even glance backward at the sound of his name; he didn't give my warnings to stop even the slightest acknowledgement.

Bobby was inside the Shipley house before Leah or I had really had time to process what he was doing. Then the front door swung shut behind him.

And the purple lights that had been glowing behind the windows went dark.

"Damn!" I half-shouted, half-whispered to myself.

I was both terrified at and resigned to the task that lay before me. Bobby might have failed to back me up when I'd faced the tree, but he'd had my back too many times when I'd been the target of kids like Matt Stefano. I couldn't leave him alone in that house.

I began to run after him when Leah grabbed my arm.

"Wait! What are you doing, Jeff?"

"Stay here," I said. "I'm going in after him."

Leah gave me her stern, determined expression. It was an expression that I had seen only a handful of times up to this point. (And oddly enough, this expression had a way of deepening my infatuation for her—even more than one of her smiles.)

"I will not 'stay here', Jeff. And I appreciate what you did back there—and other things that you've done. But if you think this means that you're going to order me around, you've got another thing coming. And besides, what do you expect me to do—stand here in the street by myself? What if something else comes along? No way; it's better if we stick together."

We were losing time, as Bobby had already been inside the Shipley house for the better part of a minute. I could see that this was an argument that I wasn't going to win.

And Leah might have been right, for all I knew.

"Okay," I said. "Come on."

Leah and I started across the lawn of the Shipley house. We paused only briefly as the door swung open again. Then it gaped at us like a giant maw. I saw no sign of Bobby, but nor did I see any sign of the witch, which was a minor source of relief.

"Why do you think he ran toward that house?" Leah asked me.

"I don't know."

But I thought that I did know—or at least I had some inkling. Bobby would only have run toward that house if he had seen something—or someone—that he wanted.

I walked in ahead of Leah. The interior of the Shipley house was more or less what might have been expected: It was dark, except for a small amount of moonlight and streetlight illumination that filtered in through the closed curtains and blinds. It bore the smells that all long-empty houses eventually acquire: those of dust, cleaning solutions, and mildew.

"Bobby!' I shouted. Leah called out his name, too. There was no answer.

"Let's search the house," I said. "We'll go room to room."

"We should stick together, though," Leah replied.

"Of course."

The Shipley house—like all the houses in this section of the neighborhood, wasn't especially large. In the late 1950s, builders were decades away from thinking in terms of those McMansions, which were only beginning to appear in the early 1980s, and wouldn't reach their heyday until after the turn of the century. These houses might contain no more than 1,100 or 1,200 square feet of space within their walls.

I was about to start down the adjacent hallway when I saw the woman walk through the kitchen.

She was ghostly, like Elmira had been. There—and not quite there. She had long, dark hair, tied back in a single ponytail. The apparition was of a woman who was neither old nor young—maybe thirty-five years of age.

There was a butcher knife protruding from her back, right between her shoulder blades. The back of her white nightgown was soaked with blood.

The woman's neck had also been slashed. Like Elmira's head wound, these were injuries that no human being could have sustained and survived.

Which made a queer kind of sense—given that the woman was obviously not a woman at all, but a ghost.

I was relieved when the apparition of the woman, having made her way across the kitchen, passed into the far wall and disappeared. But then I caught sight of her two children, following behind their mother.

Years later, as a student at the University of Cincinnati, I would research the murders and suicide that had taken place in the house at 1371 Applegate Drive in 1959. By the time I was in college (the late 1980s), there was still no Internet, but old newspapers could be read on microfilm. I would sit alone at one of the university library's microfilm readers, hoping that no one was looking over my shoulder. *(My interest in such an old and grisly crime would have been difficult to explain.)*

My research would eventually tell me that while Donald Shipley had ended his own life with a single gunshot to the head from a .38 special, he had dispatched his wife and two sons with a butcher knife.

Donald Shipley's sons walked across the kitchen in that state, with wounds so ghastly that I found myself forced to turn away from them. After a few more footsteps, they disappeared into the wall—into the same spot where their mother had gone.

"Did you see tha—?"

My question was cut off by the realization that Leah was no longer standing beside me. I turned frantically around in a full circle, allowing myself a few seconds of vain hope, grasping at the possibility that Leah had merely moved behind me or to the other side of me.

"Leah!" I called out her name. I hadn't heard her walk away, and I was certain that I would have heard if anything from the hidden corners of this house had come out and taken her. I had been transfixed by the three apparitions, to be sure, but for less than a full minute.

I then allowed myself to succumb to optimism—to what might be the easiest solution. I walked back to the front door, which was still ajar as Leah and I had left it. Maybe, I thought, Bobby and Leah had both gone back outside while I was mesmerized by the images of the doomed mother and her young sons. Maybe they were out there in the yard even now, waiting for me to join them so we could continue onward, and get this horrible ordeal over with.

When I stepped into the doorway and looked outside, though, I did not see either Leah or Bobby. I called out to them again, just in case they were anywhere in the immediate vicinity. I didn't believe that they would have journeyed far beyond the house without waiting for me.

I noticed a presence in the road, in front of the house, which I briefly took for either Bobby or Leah. It was neither Bobby nor Leah, though.

The witch—the same witch that had been standing in the doorway where I now stood—watched me from the middle of Applegate Drive. She gave me a wide smile, a look at those long, serrated teeth.

Then she shook her head slowly at me—as if she could read my thoughts. No—Bobby and Leah had not left the Shipley house; our time here would not be concluded so easily.

I stepped back inside the Shipley house, and closed the door behind me. I was afraid of what might be inside this house with me, but the witch and the unknown dangers outside were equally fearful. And if I went back outside, I would face it all alone. My friends were still somewhere within these walls.

I heard the door to the Shipley house click shut at almost the exact moment that I heard the voices.

My first impression was that a party was taking place in one of the house's bedrooms—as unlikely as that sounds. I heard laughter—distinctly feminine laughter.

Then I heard a semi-familiar voice call my name.

It was the voice of a girl about my own age. My first thought was that the voice belonged to Leah; but then she spoke my name again, and I was able to rule out that deduction. She was someone I knew (I thought)—but she wasn't the girl who had accompanied me into the Shipley house.

Then another girl called my name. And then came the voice of a woman who was distinctly older.

I looked down the main hall of the Shipley house. (Again, there was only one hall, given the smallness of the house.) I saw a partially open bedroom door, and a shaft of light that gave off a reddish hue.

This wasn't like the purple light that had earlier emanated from the outside windows. That light had been cold and unnatural. This light gave me an incongruously warm feeling, considering where I was. The light drew me in that direction—as did the voices of unseen girls and women.

"Jeff! Jeff! Come in here! We've been waiting for you."

I walked toward the bedroom door. I wasn't afraid anymore—not of the Shipley house, nor of the witch, nor of what might be waiting inside that bedroom.

I pushed the door open, briefly noting that the light bulb overhead burned red rather than white.

The bedroom was richly furnished: There was an antique four-poster bed, its wood decorated with carvings of...

(Goats? Satyrs? Serpents?)

And at the foot of the bed was an equally antique ottoman. The face of the ottoman was dominated by a burnished image of a goat's head. The goat's face was clenched in a snarl that you would never see on the face of an actual goat.

The carpet beneath my feet was thick, foamy, mauve in color.

And it seemed to be pulsating, churning beneath my feet.

I had to overlook the room's inexplicable décor, however—and the sensation of hands beneath the carpeting and floorboards, pushing upwards and grasping at the bottoms of my shoes. Because I was not alone—no, far from it, in fact.

"Jeff," one of them said. "We thought you'd never find your way in here."

The first one I recognized was Sheila Hunt—the prettiest, most popular girl in my seventh grade class.

Sheila was wearing an outfit that took my breath away: nothing but a bra and panties. In truth, her attire was no more revealing than the bikinis girls regularly wore during the summer. But this was *underwear*—it was shockingly and irresistibly intimate. This was a sight that I *wasn't supposed to see.* And *Sheila Hunt*, to boot.

I had never seen a real live girl or woman in her underwear, of course. There was no Internet pornography in those days—even of the softcore variety; and at the age of twelve, magazines like *Playboy* and *Penthouse* were difficult to come by. My father didn't keep such things around the house, to the best of my knowledge (though the fatherless Bobby occasionally acquired such contraband from unknown sources.)

That was, however, the last era of printed, mass-distributed catalogs from stores like Sears and JC Penney. My mother kept the catalogs in our family room. On many occasions since I'd entered this curious and desirous new phase concerning girls, I'd pretended to search through the catalogs for BB guns and video games, all the while taking furtive looks at the women's underwear sections.

Sheila Hunt was inclined on the bed, her elbows resting on two velvety-looking, dark red pillows.

Sheila Hunt was far from alone. The other girls were all ones I knew: There were Missy Davis and Laura Robinson from the seventh grade; Julie Price and Allison Sweeny from the eighth grade.

They were all lounging on the bed or standing around the room, and all clad in their underwear—underwear, I was sure, that I had recently seen in JC Penney and Sears catalogs.

"Jeff Schaeffer, you're going to be late for class!"

That came from one of the two women in the room, Mrs. Jenkins and Miss Powell. Both were teachers at St. Patrick's. Mrs. Jenkins and Miss Powell both taught the younger kids at St. Patrick's—so they weren't my teachers. But I'd noticed them on many occasions. They were in their late twenties (well, Mrs. Jenkins may have been in her early thirties); and both had made numerous romps through my imagination. At various times, I had fantasized about being seduced by one of them—knowing full well that it was never going to happen.

But it seemed to be happening now.

Miss Powell and Mrs. Jenkins were dressed as revealingly as the younger girls. They wore makeup—dark blue eye shadow and lipstick that made their lips appear glossy and wet, almost like they were made of liquid.

I took in the entire scene—the girls and women all dressed as they were, all of them looking at me. The lipstick and the makeup, their voices warm and beckoning.

"You can do anything you want," Miss Powell said, favoring me with a smile that her fifth grade students would certainly never see. "You can do anything you want to any of us."

That was the invitation that caused my body to respond, involuntarily and urgently. Since the late 1990s, Viagra and similar drugs have not only desensitized our culture to the concept of the male erection, they have also led many people to believe that every other man has trouble with them.

That might be true for men of a certain age. But believe me, when you are twelve or thirteen years old, erections happen without any intervention or effort on your part.

And unlike later in life, they are no joking matter. In fact, they are often accompanied by deep embarrassment and even shame.

They caught sight of my reaction. Half of them started lasciviously laughing then, and the other half issued the sorts of invitations that I had so often fantasized about—alone in my room at night when the rest of the family was asleep.

I reached down and covered myself with both hands. Then I forced myself to look away from them, to a nearby empty corner of the room.

This is not real, I told myself. *None of this is real. It can't be.*

Perhaps the jolt of shame over my erection was exactly what I needed to snap me out of the elaborate illusion that had been spun for me. I suddenly grasped the enormity of the deception. How could Sheila Hunt, Miss Powell, and all the others possibly be here in this bedroom inside the Shipley house?

They couldn't be, obviously.

This was the house's way of lulling me to sleep, or tricking me into dropping my ordinary defenses—which would be reckless in this environment.

"You're not real," I said, facing them again. "None of you are real."

"But Jeff," Miss Powell said. "Of course we're real! Aren't we, Sheila?"

The thing that was impersonating Miss Powell still looked like her, more or less; but her voice was throatier now, not quite as convincing. And Sheila nodded her head woodenly in response to the question, as if she were a marionette on a handful of strings.

"You're not real," I repeated.

"Of course we're real!" Miss Powell shrieked, as the light bulb over my head went suddenly dark. But Miss Powell wasn't Miss Powell anymore. She was the witch that I had heretofore seen only at a distance. She was clad in black robes, and her grayish, milky eyes were spiderwebbed with veins. She curled her lip back, giving me yet another look at those hideous teeth.

"You're not real!" I was shaking violently now.

The witch responded with a deep, angry hiss. Then she ran past me, in a blur of putrid odor, dust, and the coarse feel of her black attire. In the second when she passed, I had an unanticipated image: the witch's garments had been plucked from graveyard corpses, and sewn together to form her robes.

Where had that image come from, I wondered. Even more, why had she spared me?

Perhaps I had temporarily altered the balance of power. The witch had spun an elaborate illusion and pulled me into it, but it had taxed her considerably. And I had seen through the deception—broken it, in fact.

You see, I thought to myself. *These things that we've been encountering tonight—they might be dangerous; they might even be capable of killing you. But they aren't all-powerful. They can be defeated.*

Maybe they can even be destroyed.

It might have been the sin of hubris—but this last thought was oddly exhilarating, despite the overall situation.

The bedroom was almost completely dark now, a small amount of moonlight entered between the slats in the blind of the room's only window. The four-poster bed and the ottoman were gone—they had been nothing but components of the illusion. And the floor beneath my feet was not carpet, but hardwood.

But I still wasn't alone in the room—even though the girls and women were gone, and the witch was gone.

I became aware of a series of chirps, clicks, and squeaks. Something skittered over one of my feet.

I took two frantic steps backward and then looked down—in that order. The floor space where I had been standing was churning with mice, crickets, cockroaches, and other vermin. Two large rats grappled for position among the other filthy creatures; their beady eyes reflected the scant moonlight.

Why had these animals—the vermin that hide in crevices, beneath rocks, and in the filth left over by humans—congregated here, in this room? Perhaps, I speculated, they had formed the raw materials by which the witch had orchestrated her deception.

I backed out of the room, shuddering, and closed the door behind me.

I still had to find my friends, of course. I found Leah one bedroom over.

I almost missed her. Leah was kneeling on one knee in one of the house's two secondary bedrooms. She was staring at a swarming mass of insects, mice, and similar vermin with great fascination. This horde, like the horde in the other bedroom, contained at least one scabrous rat.

I had never known Leah to be excessively inclined in what they call the "girly girl" direction. But neither was I, for that matter—and I had grown squeamish before a similarly amassed concentration of lower-end fauna.

I watched as a snake slithered across Leah's outstretched calf without her even noticing it. There aren't many poisonous snakes in Ohio, so it was probably just a garter snake.

But still.

"Leah!" I shouted. "What are you doing?"

"Can't you see?" she asked, turning briefly to face me. "Look at it. There's a dollhouse, and a unicorn, and a tea set. A real china tea set!"

Leah's eyes bore a glassy quality that suggested intoxication or mesmerization. Her mouth hung half open and slack. She wasn't quite asleep, but she wasn't fully awake, either.

"Leah, what's wrong with you?"

But I knew, didn't I? The exact same thing—my own peculiar strain of it—had been "wrong with me" only a few minutes ago.

"*I want to stay!*" she said, insistently.

It was Leah who had spoken; there was absolutely no doubt about that. But this version of Leah seemed much younger. I might have been talking to a girl of seven or eight, versus a girl who would be starting high school in a little more than a year.

I walked into the room. As I moved forward, I could feel crickets, beetles, and cockroaches crunching beneath my feet. I thought I stepped on a mouse too; I felt its tiny ribcage burst, I heard it give out a frantic, dying shriek.

I knelt in the muck and grabbed Leah by the shoulders.

"Leah," I said. "This is no good."

"I want to stay here," she said insistently—still dazed.

"You can't." I was whispering in her ear now.

Then I looked up and saw the witch staring at us through the slats in the room's single window. Her eyes met mine and she smiled. I felt a fresh shiver go through my body.

Leah didn't notice the witch, of course. She was still looking at the dirty, swarming things, imagining them to be the idealized trappings of the childhood that was slipping away from her every day: dollhouses, unicorns, tea sets—endless summer days that challenged neither her innocence, nor her sense of security.

"I don't want to grow up," she said.

"But Leah," I said. "We can't stay here forever. We have to move on, right?" I couldn't believe that Leah—of all people—was nervous about the future. I'd thought that I was the only one who was nervous about the future: I was plenty comfortable where I was, after all—where I'd always been.

What kind of a person would I become beyond the age of twelve? Would high school, and then adulthood, shred me to pieces? Would anyone—except my parents, of course—ever love me?

"Aren't you looking forward to it all?" I asked her. "I mean: high school, and college, and whatever comes after all of that?"

I stopped myself. Even under these circumstances, it seemed fanciful to contemplate life that far in advance. High school alone—barely two years away—seemed a vista that stretched on forever. Any consideration of what might lie beyond that would be impossibly speculative.

"I guess so," she said, though her heart wasn't in her response. But I did at least have the impression now that I was getting through to her, that she realized who it was talking to her in that room.

I permitted myself another glance up at the window: The witch was still leering in at us from just outside.

And then I brought my face even with Leah's. I kissed her full on the lips. It was a chaste kiss, in the big scheme of things, but it was one of my first.

I had played spin-the-bottle once in the sixth grade, during a classmate's birthday. His name was Wayne Harrigan; and his birthday party had been one of the first coed parties among my circle of friends and acquaintances.

The party had been staged in the basement of Wayne's house; and his parents had given us several hours without adult supervision. Someone had come up with the idea of playing spin-the-bottle. After a few rounds, most of the girls had chickened out; but I managed to kiss two girls before the game ended: Mindy Thompson and Kelly Greene.

I had never kissed a girl like this, though: spontaneously, risking rejection and consequences. I would not have had the courage to do so only a few days before. But after all that had happened tonight, my normal fears seemed brought down to size. I knew that they would regain their places in my mind later; but for now, I was stronger than they were.

Leah kissed me back. I could taste the Juicy Fruit gum that she had been chewing only a short while ago. Her mouth was warm and moist; and the kiss flooded me with heat, even under the circumstances.

"That was nice," she said, gently breaking the kiss and our embrace.

What I had done seemed to have broken the spell. Leah looked down at the hideous things on the floor. She gasped and stood up suddenly, brushing crickets and probably a few spiders from her legs. I stood up, too, though I was still torn between horror and a budding sense of desire, now partially fulfilled. I had kissed Leah. I had done it. And she had kissed me back.

"We've got to get out of this room," I told her.

She looked down at the floor. "You think?"

My eyes returned to the window. The witch was still there— scowling at us now.

"Come on." I took her hand and we departed, out into the hall.

We both heard Bobby yelling in the adjacent bedroom. He wasn't yelling in fear. His tone, rather, suggested anger and what might be described as a pleading desperation.

Leah and I took only a few steps down the hall and we saw him in the next room over. This bedroom, like the one we had just come from, faced the tumescent moon, and light filtered in through the slats in the blinds. Bobby's form was half bathed in moonlight. I could see the expression on his face. Bobby seemed to be lost in a trance, as Leah had been. Whereas Leah had been happy, though, Bobby was clearly in pain.

"Dad, come home!" he shouted. "All the other kids have dads. *Jeff* has a dad!"

I was taken aback by this remark. I had always assumed that I envied Bobby more than Bobby had ever envied me. Prior to the past few hours, Bobby had always been brave, whereas I had shrunk away from confrontations. He was decisive where I wavered.

But now Bobby was revealing that he envied me what I (truth be told) usually took for granted: A stable home with two parents. My dad wasn't perfect; he didn't always understand me, and he often didn't seem to try. I never had to question whether he would be there, though. I never had to wonder if he would take off someday, never to return.

I had met Bobby's father on a handful of occasions, and Bobby so often talked about him. Bobby's dad, younger than mine both in age and in spirit, seemed like a big kid himself. He talked about getting drunk and chasing after women. He treated Bobby more like a younger confidant than his son—when he was around to interact with Bobby at all, that was.

These were weighty observations, to be sure. However, I wasn't sure what relevance they had now, and why Bobby might be calling out to his father. The last time Bobby had heard from his father, he had been in Pittsburgh, living with a new girlfriend.

I quickly scanned the floor of this bedroom: There were no insects, no mice, no crawling things.

Then I noticed the shrunken, gnome-like creature in the far corner of the room. Perhaps four feet tall, it had pale, mottled gray skin, wolfish yellow eyes, and long, upright, tapered ears.

The creature was staring at Bobby, smiling slightly. The mouth came open. Like the witch, the gnome had a mouthful of serrated teeth.

Did Bobby believe that this thing was his father? Apparently he did. Why else would he address the creature so?

"Bobby!" I called out. I was standing in the doorway of the bedroom. Leah was standing right behind me, one hand on my shoulder.

Bobby appeared not to have heard me. Without warning, he let loose a loud, agonized wail, as if in physical pain. He walked into the corner of the room opposite the creature's position, sat down and placed his legs at forty-five degree angles.

Bobby burst into tears. He buried his face in his hands.

"Not fair!" he sobbed. *"You're not being fair!"*

The gnome-like thing took a step toward Bobby. Bobby, lost in his illusion and crying into his open hands, was heedless of the threat.

I had to get him out of there, I realized. I ran into the room to where Bobby was seated, and did my best to ignore the gnome. Though small in stature, the gnome was frightening in its intensity.

I seized one of Bobby's arms. He looked up at me, his face wet. He was clearly surprised to see me there.

"Bobby! You have to get up. You have to get out of here."

That was when I heard a low, croaking sound. I looked to the other side, away from Bobby, and saw the gnome advancing on both of us, with that slow deliberation that seemed to be the creature's trademark.

"Stand up, Bobby!"

I gave his arm a firm yank, and Bobby clambered to his feet, me half pulling him.

Then there was another loud croak. I involuntarily glanced at the gnome: The thing was staring at me now. Its yellow eyes widened with what must have been implacable hatred.

"Come on, Bobby!" Bobby was now standing, though a bit unsteadily. I grabbed him by his shirt and pulled him around, so that he was facing me.

"Come on!" I repeated.

Bobby allowed me to pull him in the direction of the bedroom's doorway. By the time we were halfway there, he had begun to actively move under his own power.

Behind us, the gnome that had been impersonating Bobby's father croaked furiously.

Once in the hallway, Bobby began to wipe his eyes. He was suddenly self-conscious of the fact that he had been crying. I sympathized with him, but he—well, we didn't have time right now.

"Let's move!" I said to Leah and Bobby. "We have to get out of this house!"

The house at 1371 Applegate was a small house, as I have said, so it was only a few paces to the front door. I let my friends run ahead of me. We pushed through the door and found ourselves out on the front porch. I pulled the door closed behind us.

I heard a rustling in the adjacent bushes, which were easily tall enough to conceal a full-grown man. Bobby and Leah heard the rustling, too.

The gnome? The witch? Or maybe something even worse? Any of these were possible.

"Go!" I shouted at Bobby and Leah. I gave them both a gentle push. There was no law that said we had to stand around and wait for it to show itself, whatever it was.

We walked quickly away from the house where—a decade before we were born—a deranged man named Donald Shipley had killed his wife and two children.

We were out on the blacktop of Applegate Drive before either Bobby or Leah spoke.

"Now where?" Bobby asked. Despite his ordeal in the house, Bobby's tone suggested resentment rather than any variety of gratitude or relief. I suspected that he knew—or at least sensed—that

Leah and I had witnessed him in a reduced state, a vulnerable position.

And how else could you describe a twelve-year-old boy who collapses into tears in a corner, while temporarily under the illusion that some monstrosity is his father?

That hadn't been a shining moment for Bobby, however you sliced it. Bobby would be feeling humiliated and defensive right now. But I didn't have time to make allowances for those feelings at the moment. Those feelings would have to be dealt with later.

"We move forward," I said. "We keep going to the end of the route we take every Halloween—which will eventually bring us back to where we started. "Then," I said, "I'll get my mom or my dad to take you home, so you won't have to walk that extra distance by yourself."

This had been the wrong thing to say; I knew this as soon as the words escaped my mouth. But we didn't have time for those emotions at the moment. Bobby looked at me as if to protest, then looked away and nodded.

"I suppose you're right," he said. "At least—I don't see any other way."

"No," Leah agreed. "There really is no alternative."

"Let's go then," I said. I began walking down Applegate Drive, along the path that would eventually take us home. I didn't look back: somehow I was confident that Leah and Bobby would follow me, and they did.

"Some of these houses have lights on in the windows," Leah observed.

"You want to go trick-or-treating?" Bobby asked. "We don't even have our candy bags anymore."

"No, silly," she shot back. "But someone inside one of these houses might be willing to help us."

"Or they might be another one of them," Bobby countered.

There was a petty part of me that secretly delighted in seeing this new friction between Leah and Bobby. It was wrong, I knew; both of them were my friends. I shouldn't want to see them snapping at each other. Moreover, we needed to stick together. Our trial was likely far from over.

We had been walking no more than five minutes when we saw the figure running toward us in the street. The figure was male— older than us, perhaps in his late teens or early twenties.

At first I thought him to be a ghost. But as he approached, his appearance took on a distinctly human aspect. He was taller than any of us, but not of supernatural proportions.

More than anything, though, was the fact that he was gasping for air as he ran. Ghosts, it was easy to figure, didn't require oxygen. They wouldn't become winded when running.

Then there was another observation: The person running toward us was obviously scared to death. That told me immediately that he was on our side, not theirs. I felt no need to flee from him; and neither did Leah or Bobby, apparently. We stopped walking, though. He was making a beeline for our position.

"Don't go down there!" he shouted. As the young man came fully into view, I was able to discern his identity: This was Jimmy Wilson. He was a recent graduate of Bishop Stallings High School. He lived in our neighborhood. Jimmy was presently a commuting student at the University of Cincinnati, majoring in engineering or mathematics, something highbrow like that.

In the pecking order of teens and adolescents, most high school kids leave junior high students alone. Even among the bullies, there is no prestige for the sixteen-year-old bully to gain from intimidating a twelve-year-old. Conventional wisdom held that you didn't become targets of the high school bullies until you entered high school yourself.

Still, we knew which ones to watch out for, which ones to give a wide berth as a precautionary measure. Jimmy Wilson, fortunately, wasn't one of those. None of us knew him really well. But nor did we consciously avoid him. He was vaguely aware of our existence, as we were vaguely aware of his. Once in a while he would wave to us as he was driving through the neighborhood in his forest green '74 Chevy

Nova. I might have spoken to him half a dozen times prior to this night, all of these occasions being very brief verbal exchanges.

"Oh," he said, recognizing us. "Hi."

We all said hello in return. Well, Leah and I did. Bobby merely grunted.

Jimmy leaned forward with his hands on his thighs, allowing himself to rest. He was panting hard, I noticed. Had Jimmy been an athlete in high school? No, I didn't think he had been. He was tall and thin with naturally curly brown hair. He looked like the sort of kid who might have been an athlete, but he wasn't. Jimmy was more of what you'd call a "brain". In late 1980, Microsoft's now famous cofounder had not yet become a nationally known figure. But if Jimmy had known of him, he probably would have wanted to become another Bill Gates.

"Anyway," Jimmy said, looking up at us, you shouldn't go down there—that way you're going. They destroyed my car. Totally fricking trashed it!" And when Jimmy added this fact, there was real pain in his expression. He had obviously loved his forest green Chevy Nova. Either Bobby or I would have loved it, too.

"They trashed your car?" Bobby asked.

Jimmy stared back at him. "That's right."

"Who?" Leah asked. "Who messed up your car?"

Jimmy stood up and sighed. He wasn't wearing a Halloween costume, obviously, given his age. His oxford-style blue dress shirt was untucked and half unbuttoned. His jeans were stained with what might have been grease or dirt. The fabric covering his right thigh was torn, revealing a patch of very white skin that had probably never been decently tanned.

"Ronny, Larry, and Jerry," Jimmy said. "Ronald Willis, Larry Sturgis, and Jerry Ames, to be exact. Do you know who they are —or were?"

Leah, Bobby and I looked back and forth at each other. None of us had heard these names before.

"No," Jimmy said. "I guess you haven't. That was before your time, wasn't it? Before my time, too, actually. Maybe I'll have a chance to tell you about that. But right now we need to get out of here. It isn't safe around here."

Bobby snorted. "No shit, Sherlock."

Jimmy dismissed Bobby's sarcasm with a mild look of annoyance. "Have the three of you seen anything—unusual—out here tonight?" he asked.

"Have we?" Leah said. "Have we ever."

We proceeded to give Jimmy an overview of everything that had happened to us that night—and all that we had seen: the realistic gravestones that might have been nothing more than someone's sick idea of a joke, but were almost certainly something else, in retrospect. The moaning, writing bodies in the muck. Elmira and the tree. The Shipley house.

Jimmy took it all in without too much visible surprise. "It's happening again, then," he said.

"What's happening?" I asked.

"I don't exactly know," Jimmy said. "All I can tell you is that something similar happened to me about five or six years ago, when I was your age, more or less. Tell me: Have any of you been visited by this weird kid? He looks, I don't know, maybe fifteen or sixteen years old?"

"You mean the 'ghost boy?" I replied.

"Yeah. I suppose that's as good a name for him as any. Though my friends and I called him the 'dead kid'. Same thing, I guess. Well, he's been fifteen or sixteen for a long, long time."

Jimmy's revelation created more questions than it answered. The things we had been seeing and experiencing tonight—Jimmy had seen and experienced them, too. But why? And what exactly was going on?

"Who is he?" I asked. "I mean the ghost boy—the dead kid."

"I don't know," Jimmy admitted. "You want my best guess? I'd say he's some wandering ghost who found his way here, and decided to stay. Or maybe he used to live here. I don't really know.

"Say," Jimmy asked. "Do all of you believe in ghosts?"

We nervously laughed and muttered various responses that mingled bravado with gallows humor. Whatever we had believed in before this night, there could be no doubt about the matter now. Yes, we all believed in ghosts.

"Good," Jimmy said. "Because whether or not you believe in them, they believe in you. That's the important thing. Now, we need to get the hell out of here, if you'll excuse my French. We shouldn't be standing in the middle of the road here—not with Ronny, Larry, and Jerry around. I know a place not far from here where we should be safe until the danger passes—the immediate danger, that is. Follow me."

15

Without any hesitation or debate, we followed him. Jimmy Wilson was older than us, and he obviously had experience with whatever this was that was occurring tonight. He would help us, we were certain.

I realized then that we had a new leader—just as I had been growing into the role of leadership myself.

This left me with mixed feelings. On one hand, I was relieved. Now that the adrenalin rush was dissipating, I was beginning to grow seriously afraid. I might even have been going into a form of mild shock, for all I knew. That part of me was more than willing to turn over the reins of leadership, to entrust myself and my friends to the superior judgment of a quasi-adult. I didn't even bother to ask myself if we could truly trust Jimmy, if he really had our best interests at heart.

Yet another part of me wanted to chafe against Jimmy's instructions and what amounted to an usurpation. I had been doing just fine, hadn't I? I had gotten Elmira through that gate. I had gotten my friends out of the Shipley house.

Jimmy led us away from the road, taking us through several back yards. We passed by tool sheds and copses of pine, shrubbery, and maple trees. We walked by an above-ground aluminum pool that had been covered for the season weeks ago, and already sported a coating of late autumn leaves.

We saw lights on in some of the houses, but no one challenged our presence. We moved carefully and quietly, like soldiers on patrol behind enemy lines.

Still, I felt compelled to quiz Jimmy about his past experiences with these phenomena.

"You've been through this before, then"? I asked him.

"That's what I said."

"And you mentioned that you weren't the only one. You specifically said 'my friends and I', I think."

"That's right. Two guys just a few years older than me: names are Brian Dozier and Mark Hayworth. You know either of them?"

I shrugged as I negotiated a dark patch of shrubbery. I was walking alongside Jimmy. Leah and Bobby were trailing a few paces behind us. I might have heard the names before, but like all significantly older kids, Dozier and Hayworth would have moved in circles far outside my orbit. I indicated as much to Jimmy.

"Well, if you haven't met them yet, then I don't imagine you ever will," he said. "Because Mark and Brian took off—left town for college after graduation. I don't expect them to ever come back."

"You mean all this scared them off?"

"Who knows? It all happened when we were pretty young—like I said, around your age. And although we all went to Bishop Stallings together, I could never get either one of them to ever talk about it again."

I thought about Bobby and Leah, and how both of them had been in vehement denial about all of this, until the evidence became too overpowering for them to ignore or evade. After all this was over, though (and assuming that we all survived the ordeal), would my friends revert to their former stubborn silence? That possibility didn't seem out of the question, though I had more immediate concerns at the moment.

"Did you see the girl?" I asked Jimmy. "I mean Elmira."

"Yeah, I saw her," Jimmy replied, and a shadow crossed his face. "We all saw her. She wanted us to open that gate for her. But none of us did. We were too afraid of that damned tree."

"Well, Jeff opened the gate," Leah said from behind us. She had been eavesdropping, apparently. And Bobby, too.

"Yeah, old Jeff here is a regular action hero nowadays," Bobby said, reaching forward as he walked to clap me on the shoulder.

I didn't say anything. As was sometimes the case with Bobby, it was difficult to know where his joking demeanor ended and his serious side began.

I might not be an "action hero". But I had risen to a challenge that had been too much for Bobby, Jimmy, and these other two boys, Brian Dozier and Mark Hayworth. I would be lying if I said that didn't puff me up with pride. I wasn't going to say as much, though.

"Here we are," Jimmy said. He directed us to a natural enclosure formed by a small group of medium-sized trees. We were in someone's back yard, but the windows of the house were dark, suggesting that the owners wouldn't be inclined to disturb us. And besides, after all that we had faced this evening, an irate homeowner would seem like little more than an annoyance.

"We should be safe here," Jimmy elaborated. "Be careful, though, this place is covered with apples. The last thing any of us needs right now is a twisted ankle."

Jimmy punctuated this admonition with a laugh. He was right on both counts, though: The ground within the little tree enclosure was indeed covered with apples—presumably ones that had fallen prematurely, or had been rejected by whoever owned this property. And he was also correct in asserting that a mundane injury like a twisted ankle could be a disaster on a night like tonight, under circumstances such as these.

We each took a seat on the cold ground, brushing away the apples and the fallen tree leaves as much as possible. We were in a little orchard then. I was reminded once again of Elmira: She had referred to her family's apple orchard. There had been apples here on that long ago day, when Elmira ventured outside and was butchered by a roaming Shawnee war party. And there were apples here now, as Bobby, Leah, Jimmy Wilson and I were fleeing from threats of a very different kind.

"Why do you think this happens?" Leah asked Jimmy. I had thought of asking him the exact same thing.

Perhaps, because Jimmy was older than us, we expected him to have all the answers, to somehow possess knowledge that was hopelessly beyond our reach. However, Jimmy's response suggested that he was just as confused as we were.

"You'd might as well ask, 'why do plane crashes happen?' Or what about car wrecks, or heart attacks? Or what about nuclear war?"

"Nuclear war?" Leah queried. "What nuclear war?"

"Well," Jimmy allowed. "There hasn't been a nuclear war yet—not unless you want to count Hiroshima and Nagasaki, that is. But the USA and the Soviet Union are both loaded for bear and armed to the teeth. Between us, we've got enough nuclear missiles to destroy the world like a dozen times. Did you kids know that?"

We all shrugged. We might have heard that somewhere.

"Anyway," Jimmy went on, "if Reagan wins the election next week, there will probably be a war between the United States and the USSR. You can bank on that." Jimmy paused to look around us. "Then none of this will make any difference, anyway."

I glanced over at Bobby and saw him roll his eyes. I couldn't entirely disagree with the implied sentiment. Why was Jimmy speculating about a war that might or might not come, when we faced all these very real and imminent threats? Neither the Soviet Union nor Ronald Reagan (nor Jimmy Carter for that matter) had destroyed his forest green Nova—the one that was so much the envy of the younger boys in the neighborhood, and probably some of the adults, too. And the things in the Shipley house—whatever they'd been—they had had nothing to do with elections or geopolitics.

"Anyway," Jimmy said, perhaps sensing our impatience. "Let me tell you about Ronald, Larry and Jerry, because you definitely need to watch out for them.

. . .

"IT WAS A LONG TIME AGO," Jimmy began. "Back in 1962—yes, I think that was the year. Before any of you kids were born. I was only a year old then."

"You can cut the 'kids' crap," Bobby said. "If you were born in nineteen-sixty-one, then you're only seven years older than us. It's not like you're our parents' age."

"Do you want to hear the story, or not?" Jimmy said. "Because I really think that you need to know about this."

"It's okay," I said, shooting a look at Bobby, and then at Jimmy. "Please, go on: It's been a long night for everyone here, hasn't it?"

"You can say that again." Jimmy nodded. "All right. Here goes.

"Their names—when they were alive that is, were Ronald Willis, Larry Sturgis, and Jerry Ames. They all went to Youngman High School. The school was new back in those days, believe it or not. But I don't know if any of them graduated. They were all nineteen or so when their car crashed into the retaining wall on Aicholtz Road, over by Eastgate Mall."

"Wait a minute," I said. "There isn't any retaining wall on Aicholtz Road."

"That's because they removed it," Jimmy explained. "No, not because of the crash. They took out the wall in the early 1970s, when they completed this stretch of I-275."

Interstate 275, or I-275, is the Cincinnati bypass, the beltway that goes around the Greater Cincinnati area, dipping into northern Kentucky in the south, and extending into Indiana at its westernmost point. The first ground was broken on I-275 in the early 1960s. The beltway wasn't completed until the early 1970s. It had been completed since Leah, Bobby, and I could remember, but Jimmy would be old enough to remember the days when the Interstate ended just short of Withamsville.

Over the past decade, the countryside around Withamsville had been transitioned from farmland to the beginnings of suburban sprawl. The mall to which Jimmy referred, Eastgate Mall, was brand-new in 1980. Bobby and I liked to go there on Saturdays, when we could convince an adult to drive us. It was a place to shop for vinyl record albums, and look at the high school girls who were hopelessly beyond our reach.

"Ronald, Larry, and Jerry, were hoodlums of the old-fashioned variety," Jimmy continued. "I'm talking black leather motorcycle jackets, ducktail haircuts—the whole nine yards."

"Stop," Bobby said, interrupting again. "How do you know all this?"

"Because I saw them tonight. Like I told you. Like I'm trying to explain to you."

"But 1962 was almost twenty years ago. I can do the math, you know. That would make these guys what—forty years old?"

Jimmy shook his head slowly at Bobby. "You don't get it, do you? These guys aren't forty years old, any more than that girl Elmira is a hundred and sixty or whatever. Ronny, Larry, and Jerry are still nineteen years old, and I suspect that they'll be nineteen years old in the year two thousand—when all of us will be—jeez, I don't even want to think about how old I'll be then."

"Whatever, man. Okay—finish your story. Please." It was difficult to tell whether the last word had been intended in sincerity or sarcasm.

Bobby sighed and leaned back against the trunk of the apple tree that he had staked out. Was he being deliberately obtuse? Was he sliding back into comfortable denial—even after everything that he had seen tonight?

"Where was I?" Jimmy began again, more than a little annoyed now. "Oh, yeah: Ronny, Larry and Jerry were your typical small-town toughs, like the kind that you see in those old movies starring James Dean. What was the name of that film? Do any of you know, offhand?"

"*Rebel without a Cause,*" Leah provided. I was growing annoyed myself by this time, with Jimmy's many tangents, and his meandering style. What difference did it make—the name of an old movie?

"Yeah, that's it," Jimmy agreed. "Except I think that the James Dean character was probably a lot nicer. There was nothing nice about these three. Jerry Ames was charged with rape—I know that for a fact, as I heard it from some of the old-timers—but the charges were dropped when the victim refused to testify."

"That's awful!" Leah said indignantly.

Jimmy nodded. "Yep. It was. It *is*. But those were different times, you know? And I imagine what happened was that the girl was afraid for her life. And probably not without reason. Ronald and Larry put a kid in the hospital when they were still in high school. They were bad apples. Not only bad apples—but thoroughly mean, from what I've been told. And—" Jimmy swallowed hard, "from what I've seen more recently. Not the sort of guys you would want to mess with—alive or dead."

I was half-expecting Bobby to make an expression of sarcasm or skepticism at this point. Thankfully, he kept quiet.

"They were always in trouble with the law. I don't know what exact charges—other than the rape charges that were dropped—but they had acquired a reputation.

"One night, so the story goes, Ronald, Larry, and Jerry robbed a store along the main drag in Withamsville. It was a burglary, I think —not an armed robbery. But somebody saw them, called the cops, and pretty soon they were running for their freedom. But where would they have gone? This wasn't the wild West, not even then." Jimmy chuckled.

"Anyway, they ran for it—in their old Mercury Montclair. Except I guess it wasn't that old then, was it? And they ended up crashing into that retaining wall that used to stand at the north end of Aicholtz Road. All three of them were killed on impact." Jimmy chuckled nervously. "So they never got arrested, I guess."

"What happened to the bodies?" Bobby asked.

Jimmy nodded, as if he had been merely waiting to get to this point.

"They were bad kids, by any measure, but they all came from respectable families. They're buried over in the Mount Moriah Cemetery—though not exactly together, all of them are in the old section of the graveyard. You could probably find their graves, if you wanted to."

I gave an involuntary shudder. The Mount Moriah Cemetery had been receiving bodies since the early 1800s, and it was almost full, I thought I had heard someone say. It was a peaceful but still somehow spooky place, frequented by crows and made obscure by an internal forest of ancient pine trees. One end of the cemetery abutted Ohio Pike. I had been past the cemetery hundreds of times. I never gave the place a second thought. I had not yet had any encounters with Ronald Willis, Larry Sturgis, or Jerry Ames, but it was nevertheless disturbing to think that these three were buried in that all too familiar place.

"I think you can figure out the rest," Jimmy said. "Those were three guys who decided that they couldn't stay dead—*wouldn't* stay dead. They aren't out and about all the time, but they come out at certain times—when the borders are thin and the conditions are right."

I thought again about what Mr. Snyder had said about the *liminal time.*

"Did you see them before?" I asked. "I mean—the last time this happened to you?"

"No. You want my opinion? I think that all of this is nothing more than a brief gap between those 'borders' I mentioned. I think that all those things that are out and about tonight—the dead kid (the 'ghost boy', to you), that girl on her swing and that horrible tree, and," he sighed, "Ronny, Larry and Jerry—I think that they're around all the time; but we can only see them from time to time. I think there are forces like that everywhere. Maybe there are more of them around here than in other places, because this is a place where the boundaries are so thin." Jimmy looked up into the night sky, contemplatively. The full moon was off to our left; and it cast long shadows amid the apple trees. "But I don't really know."

"Well, I'm glad we found you," I said. Even though I had ambivalent feelings about Jimmy assuming leadership over the group, I felt it was appropriate to explicitly acknowledge him. Jimmy Wilson had been through this before, I reasoned—and he had lived through it. With his help, maybe *we* would live through it, too.

I decided that it would be okay for me to speak for all of us. "We appreciate you sticking with us."

Jimmy stood up abruptly, and began brushing off his pants. "No," he said. "I—I'm sorry; but that isn't going to be possible. Not beyond this point."

"What?" Bobby and Leah also made sounds of protest. Jimmy had given us the distinct impression that the four of us were a team now —at least until we got through this.

"Based on what you told me," Jimmy said, "the curse is on you this time. Seven years ago it was my problem."

"And now it's *not your problem* anymore? Is that it?" Bobby challenged him.

"Hell of a way to put it," Jimmy retorted.

"Yes, a hell of a way to put it," Leah repeated, clearly disappointed with the older boy.

"Look," Jimmy said. "It comes down to this: We need to separate. When we stick together like this, we form a bigger target." He pointed a finger at me. "The curse is on you this time. And probably your friends, too, now, since they have such a close connection to you. It was the same way for Mark, Brian and me. But me—well, I don't have a close connection to any of you. I mean, I know you and all; you kids seem nice enough. But ..."

"You couldn't stick with us just until we reached our homes?" Leah asked. "We could go straight there."

Leah was wrong, of course: We couldn't go straight home. If we tried to retrace our steps, a progressively more deadly presence would challenge us at each milestone. It would be much easier to go forward rather than backward. But Leah was feeling the desperation and resentment of a twelve-year-old girl who had been trained to see every significantly older person as a benefactor and protector.

Jimmy paused, obviously mulling the matter over.

"No," he said finally, shaking his head. "It's not my curse. Not my curse."

"Then what destroyed your car?" Bobby asked, "if this isn't 'your curse'?"

"Do you want my opinion?"

"Yeah, that was pretty much why I asked you."

"Think of this as like a storm," Jimmy said. "This storm is here mostly because of you three, but I happened to drive through it. And I had been through it before, so maybe that made me more susceptible to it. I don't know. Anyway—my car is trashed, and I need to get home myself. I've got to be going."

Jimmy started off. He turned back, and for a moment I half-believed that he might have reconsidered.

"You three, please don't try to follow me, okay? Let's not play games."

"We aren't interested in following you," Bobby said, leaning back against his tree. "Go."

"All right. Well—good luck to the three of you."

"Thanks a million," Bobby replied.

"One last thing," I interjected. I turned toward Jimmy. "Let me ask you a question."

"Shoot."

"This stuff—it isn't just a big illusion. It's all real, isn't it?"

Jimmy nodded and replied grimly, "Oh yes. It's all very real. It destroyed my car. It—it could kill you, I'm pretty sure."

With that Jimmy was gone—for real this time. He turned resolutely away from the little enclosure of trees and walked off into the darkness. He quickly disappeared from our view. We heard his footsteps for a few seconds longer, and then there was no trace of him.

"Well," Leah began, "Now what?"

I stood up. "We're back to where we were," I said. "All we have to do is walk in the direction of the road, and continue onward as we were before."

"What about those dead kids—Ronny, Larry and Jerry? They're probably out there still, you know."

"Probably," I agreed. "But they were out there before. And we've already seen plenty of bad things out here tonight. So nothing has changed."

"Jeff's right," Bobby said. He stood up with a sigh and brushed away whatever dirt, grass, and leaves had clung to his pants. "We can't just stay here all night. And we can't count on Jimmy Wilson. What a wuss."

That seemed to settle matters—at this step, at least. We set off in the direction of the road, past the tool shed that belonged to this property, and then past the house and toward the road.

As we walked by the tool shed, I noticed an ax propped against the outer wall of the little wooden building. The item had probably been overlooked by the owner, who might have been in a hurry on the last day he used it.

Something told me to take the ax with me. I had never shoplifted, and I felt a brief feeling of guilt. But it was a *very* brief feeling. I might need the axe in a matter of life or death; and I could return it later—*if* everything turned out okay.

16

The three of us were out on the road now and we resumed walking. None of us were carrying Halloween bags anymore, but I was carrying an ax. No doubt I looked strange, but conventional measures of strangeness had long since become irrelevant.

Speaking of strange, the transformation that had taken place within me tonight did not escape my notice. Only a few days ago, I had been cowering against the wall of St. Patrick's school, terrified into abject submission by Matt Stefano. And here I was now, walking down a street in my neighborhood carrying an ax. I fancied myself a little like the eponymous lead character in the movie *Mad Max*, the Mel Gibson film that had catapulted Gibson to international fame the previous year.

But how deep did this transformation go? And how permanent would it be? I had done some uncharacteristically brave things tonight, that much was true; but would I be my same cowardly self on Monday, when Matt Stefano cornered me in the schoolyard?

Speaking of Matt Stefano: What would I do if I ran into him right now, with this ax in my hand? If the older, larger boy threatened me, would I use the makeshift weapon as a way to even the odds?

It was a chilling thought, and one that I dared not contemplate. This was twenty years, more or less, before two teenage psychopaths in Littleton, Colorado would change the nature of school violence forever. Two decades before Columbine, no one—neither adults nor students—seriously contemplated the idea of well-mannered suburban kids doing real violence. The ax in my hand meant power, but it was a frightening power, and a power that could be utilized only at great cost.

No—I decided, I would not use the ax on Stefano, even if he showed up again tonight. The ax was to be used against threats of a different nature.

I was in the middle of these thoughts when I felt Bobby tug my shoulder. He signaled to me that he wanted to talk privately. I nodded and allowed Leah to advance a few paces beyond us.

"You're looking good tonight," Bobby said, in a voice low enough that Leah would be unlikely to hear. "You're showing yourself strong. I'll be honest, Schaeffer: I didn't think you had that in you."

I felt my face turn red. What was Bobby talking about, really? I assumed that the humiliation of having cried in the presence of Leah and me still stung.

"Listen," I began, "about what happened in that house—"

I needed to tell Bobby that it was no big deal, that he had been tricked by the presences inside the Shipley house, that it hadn't been a fair fight at all. I wanted to tell Bobby that none of us had done very well in there. I still recalled my raw lust before the illusion of the girls and the women. The forces inside that house—they had known our weaknesses and exploited them.

But Bobby was having none of this.

"Forget about it. This isn't me I'm talking about. I'm talking about you," he whispered. "I saw you change. And I'm not the only one."

Bobby tilted his head toward Leah, who was now a fair distance ahead of us.

She stopped suddenly in the road and looked to either side. She might have heard us talking, but she couldn't have deciphered the words, I was sure.

Leah turned fully around and looked at us.

"Hey, you guys. What are you doing? This is no time to play hide-and-seek."

"You just walk too fast for us," Bobby retorted. He smiled and clapped me on the shoulder. "Come on Schaeffer, let's double-time it up to Leah."

Leah stood her ground while Bobby and I dutifully jogged up to where she was standing.

"You guys are nuts," she said, shaking her head. "After all that has happened.

And with that, we all began walking again.

Some of the houses that we passed by were totally dark. This might have meant that they were submerged beneath the spell that had given rise to so many horrors this night. On the other hand, it might have meant that the owners of the houses were simply gone for the evening, or had turned off the lights in an effort to discourage trick-or-treaters.

Speaking of trick-or-treaters—we saw no more of them at this stage. I half suspected that we might have stayed out past the allotted time for trick-or-treat; but I knew better. We hadn't been out that long. There should still have been some late stragglers, at any rate.

Other houses had lights in the windows. Theoretically, we could have stopped at any one of them; but we had no way of knowing who and what would be behind any given door.

And besides, that wasn't the point. This was a journey that we had to finish. Taking refuge in someone's house would only delay the inevitable.

I had a crude game plan for getting us home, too: We were about halfway through our normal Halloween route, maybe a little more.

I was daring to trust that this would all work out. We had made it this far; and we would make it the rest of the way home, if only we could evade these things out here for a little longer. While these forces were formidable, they were clearly not all-powerful.

I was walking evenly with Leah and Bobby now. As inconspicuously as possible, I raised the ax in my hand, appreciating its heft. (I did not want to appear to be showing off or grandstanding.) When I got home, where the world would hopefully be normal again, I would stow the ax somewhere—probably in my father's woodpile. Then I would find a way to return it. Yes, that would be a good thing: to have the time and the space to worry about a mundane problem like the return of a pilfered ax.

"Oh, man," Bobby said suddenly. "Get a look at that, will you?"

We all saw the forest green '74 Chevrolet Nova—or rather, what was left of it.

Jimmy Wilson had loved that car, and it had been the object of much envy around the neighborhood. No one, however, would ever drive this car again.

The damage was so vast, it was difficult to take it all in at once.

The windshield had been smashed into a thousand tiny fragments. Shards of glass still clung to the frame, of course, but most of the windshield was scattered all about the pavement. All four tires had been slashed. There were dents all around the body: not shallow dents, but the deep sort of dents that could only be made with a sledgehammer or another heavy bludgeoning tool. The hood was a mess of scratches, and, I saw, some deep punctures that went clear through the metal.

Obscenities were spray-painted on the hood as well, along with a crude drawing of both male and female genitalia. Ronald, Jerry, and Larry would be in middle age if they had been alive today; they had been dead for twenty years. But they were still teenage hoodlums. For some reason, that made them all the more terrifying. *Supernatural versions of Matt Stefano*, I thought.

The front driver's side door had been left open, and looked to be askew on its hinges. The upholstery of the front seat had been torn as with a boxcutter or butcher knife.

"That car might possibly be drivable," Bobby said, appraising the destruction. "But it's totaled for all intents and purposes. Jimmy Wilson's pride and joy is good for nothing but the scrap heap now."

Leah wasn't as interested in the car as she was in the perpetrators of the damage. She wrapped her arms around herself and said,

"Are they still around, do you think—the boys who did this damage?"

They aren't boys, I thought. *If they ever were boys, they aren't boys anymore.*

"It doesn't look like it," Bobby offered. "If they were around, I think that they would have shown themselves by now. They don't exactly seem like a shy bunch, do they?

"They're gone, I think," I said. I involuntarily raised the ax again. If the long-dead vandals were to show up, would the ax be of any use against them? I had no idea. "We should just keep moving. It isn't safe for us to stay here, and there's nothing for us to do here, anyway. Jimmy Wilson deserted us, after all. The car is his problem."

"Damn right," Bobby said, nodding.

"Okay," Leah said. "But I have a bad feeling about this."

"I have a bad feeling about the entire night," I agreed. "But we can't stop moving. Let's go."

17

We had barely walked past Jimmy's ruined Nova, it seemed, when we heard the sound of an approaching vehicle.

We had not seen any other cars for quite some time—not since all of this had begun, really. For whatever reason, it seemed that cars passed through whatever slice of reality existed just on the other side of the one we were now caught in. That would be the reality of the everyday, normal world—the one to which we would hopefully return when our long walk was over.

The engine also sounded suspicious. This was no AMC Pacer or Ford Pinto. This was a serious street car, a hot rod of some sort. It announced its approach with a deep, thunderous rumble.

"Bobby," I asked. "What kind of a car did Jimmy say those guys were driving," I swallowed, "on the night they died?"

"A Mercury Montclair."

"Does a Mercury Montclair sound like that?"

"How the heck should I know? I've never ridden in one. I don't think I've ever even seen one. They haven't been made since before we were born."

"I think we'd better get back from the road—just in case," I said.

We all stepped back from the blacktop, into the adjacent front yard. This yard, luckily, had a privacy hedgerow near the road. We wove our way through the hedgerow. In summer, the hedge would have provided pretty decent cover, even on a moonlit night like tonight. This late in the season, however, the branches of the deciduous shrubs were mostly bare; and we would be easily visible to anyone who took the time to look.

No matter. It was too late and the hedgerow was the only cover available.

In less than a minute, the car was upon us. We all sighed simultaneously when we saw what it was: It wasn't some car from the 1950s or 1960s; it was a late model Corvette—probably some middle aged man's midlife crisis car, I would reflect in later years.

We couldn't make out the Corvette's exact color in the dim light, but it was a dark color: probably a dark blue or a deep red. The Corvette rumbled past, a vehicle that was blessedly commonplace and natural. It was no threat to us.

Bobby said, "I think that's one of the '78 models. I'm almost sure of it."

"Who cares?" Leah asked with a little laugh. "Just so long as it isn't the car that belonged to—them."

The Corvette was well past us now; we could see only its red taillights. The false alarm identified, we made our way out of the hedgerow, rustling branches and some brittle brown leaves in the process.

"That could be a good sign," Leah said.

"What do you mean?" Bobby asked.

"We haven't seen any cars since things went crazy," Leah said. So she had noticed that too, then. "Except for Jimmy Wilson's totaled Nova, that is. So if we're seeing normal cars—normal traffic now—maybe that means the spell, or whatever it is, is ending."

"What makes you so sure of that?" Bobby countered.

"I'm not sure," Leah said. "It's just a guess—an *extrapolation*."

"There you go with another one of your fifty cent words," Bobby teased. He was partly right: Leah read more than any of us, and she did have a vocabulary that was more advanced than that of the typical junior high student. That was more evidence of her intelligence, her precociousness. Yet another one of the innumerable factors that had suddenly, over the course of recent months, caused me to become so infatuated with her.

Leah was usually pretty game about being teased, but she ignored Bobby's remark this time. "What do you think, Jeff, is that possible?"

"It's possible," I said. I looked at Leah and Bobby. "Anything is possible, isn't it—based on what we've seen in the past few hours?"

"But—?" Leah asked.

"But you don't think we're out of the woods yet, do you Schaeffer?"

"No."

Bobby folded his arms. "Well, I don't either. Just my two cents."

Leah regarded him with a smile that might have been admiring or ironic. I couldn't be sure.

"Let's go," I said, for the umpteenth time that night.

We continued walking again, and I began to wonder if there was a part of me that didn't even want the bad spell to end. Inside the spell, after all, I had become a different person. I was no longer the boy who always played second fiddle to Bobby Nagel, the boy whom Leah Carter probably regarded as no more than a "friend".

Despite my fear, I was the brave one who was leading my friends. They were still following me. Leah was looking at me differently tonight, with the beginnings of what I dared to appraise as admiration.

A week ago, Bobby would have been the one who received her admiring looks, but tonight I was the one.

Who would I be when all of this ended, I wondered. And if I went back to being my hapless, unassuming self, could I be happy being the old Jeff Schaeffer again?

AND THEN WE came upon our third car, the third car in less than half an hour of walking.

This one, like Jimmy Wilson's old Nova, was in a state of near total destruction. But this destruction revealed itself to be the product of long years as well as sudden violence.

The car was burned, dented, and the entire front of the chassis had been partially contracted like an accordion. It was the unmistakable sign of a catastrophic impact.

The long-ago fire had charred away most of the car's original colors, but you could still make out the red and white paint that had been applied when this vehicle rolled off an assembly line somewhere.

And that would have been many, many years ago.

"This is a really old car," Bobby said, stating the obvious. The rear end of the car, which was charred and dented though structurally intact, more or less, bore a twin set of tailfins. They hadn't made cars with tailfins for years—not since the 1950s or 1960s.

"Is this a Mercury Montclair?" Leah asked.

"I'm not one hundred percent certain," Bobby answered, "but I'd say that's a pretty good guess. Wouldn't you two?"

If we had, in fact, been bouncing back and forth between worlds tonight, then this car most definitely belonged to that other world, the world of the Shipley house and the tree that had terrorized Elmira. This car, its wild damage aside, didn't belong on a street in our neighborhood. It didn't belong in this decade.

That was about when we heard the first of the voices.

"Yo, Daddy-o! Check that out!

The voice was both near and far away, simultaneously loud and faint. It was a male voice, somewhat young, though older than us.

"Oh man, did our ride get creamed good!"

A similar voice, but distinctly that of another speaker. Then we heard the third one.

"You guys kill me, man!"

"Who's there?" I asked, looking up at the moon for some reason.

"'Who's there?'" one of the voices mimicked me in a high falsetto. This remark was followed by adolescent laughter. *"Guys, I think what we've got here is a wet rag."*

"*A bunch of squares, is what we got here!*" another one said.

"*Oh, but not all of 'em, man. Will you fellas check out the dolly?*"

"*Heeyyy, baby!*"

"*Yo, baby-o!*"

I glanced over at Leah and saw that her cheeks had reddened. These words (the sources of which were as yet unseen, coming from nowhere and all around us) could only be referring to her. They obviously weren't addressing Bobby or me.

I wanted to step in and defend her. But defend her against whom? Or what?

And more to the point: How?

"*Whadaya think, Ronny? Ain't she a little on the young side?*"

"*She looks old enough for the backseat bingo to me. I bet she's a bleeder already.*"

This remark provoked a look of dread embarrassment from Leah. "Shut up!" she stammered. I could see a few tears beginning to well in her eyes.

Leah, I realized then, was struggling with much the same transformation that I was, only a different version of it. She was an adolescent, no longer a little girl, yet not quite a woman—not yet. The reference to menstruation must have hit a sensitive spot, just as I would have been deathly embarrassed had someone referred in public to my troublesome erections—which seemed to come at every inopportune moment of late. I would see an image of a woman in a swimsuit or a negligee, I would have a lascivious thought—the wind would blow, for that matter—and the front of my pants would jut out like a tent. I recalled my experiences with the illusory girls and women in the Shipley house, how my body had responded with a mind of its own.

"Shut up!" I shouted into the night air. My attempt to defend Leah from this indignity seemed woefully inadequate. It was; I was shouting at parties whom I couldn't even see.

"*Oooohhhh...I think he just told you to 'shut up', Jerry.*"

"*Yeah, well we'll just see how he likes a knuckle sandwich.*"

"*A crispy knuckle sandwich, coming from you, Daddy-o.*"

"Shut up, man!"

"Aw, you guys kill me!"

Then the voices stopped, and I thought: *They've gone away.*

I had been able to discern from the conversation that the voices belonged to Ronald Willis, Larry Sturgis, and Jerry Ames—the three young men who had crashed their Mercury Montclair one night in 1962 while fleeing from the local police. They were ghosts, obviously, and they were presumably the ones who had trashed Jimmy Wilson's prized Nova.

But maybe they were gone now. Maybe.

Then I heard a stirring from inside the burned wreck of the Mercury Montclair. I saw a tuft of blond hair slowly rise from behind the charred steering wheel, as if the person had been somehow crouched on the floorboard below the driver's seat. The tuft of hair gradually became a face, then a set of shoulders, too.

He was around Jimmy's age. His blond hair was fashioned in a ducktail haircut, the kind that no one wore anymore. He was wearing a leather jacket—another anachronism in 1980. The leather jacket was open, and he was wearing a tee shirt underneath.

He looked more or less human, more or less alive, though his skin was paler than it should have been. And he looked mean—it was a variety of meanness that was almost unknown in kids our age, I thought. Even Matt Stefano would have been afraid of him.

Then another similarly dressed boy pushed himself up in the front driver's seat. He had black hair, also in a ducktail. Another one arose in the backseat; his hair was reddish-blond.

"We were about to split for the night," said the one behind the blackened steering wheel. "But I'm glad we decided to stay."

I held up the ax, as if to show them that I wasn't afraid. I was plenty afraid, though. I was terrified.

"Aw, a wet rag, that one," said the young man in the back seat.

"Yeah, Ronny, why don't you show him who's boss!"

I had figured out now that "Ronny"—Ronald Willis—must be the one behind the steering wheel. He looked at me malevolently, his eyes strangely alive, and yet somehow not alive.

Then a cockroach emerged from Ronny's mouth, and then another. He looked down, briefly annoyed, and absently wiped them away.

"We don't get out often," said the boy in the back seat. "We should take the dolly while we're here."

That seemed to fix their plan. The doors of the crashed Mercury Montclair opened—both front doors, and the door on the driver's side in the back. The doors were only half affixed to the car, they were burned and misshaped by the impact that had killed these three. The doors, therefore, came open fitfully, unevenly, with a series of loud metallic creaks and groans.

All three of them were standing outside the wreck of the car now. It was then that the more tangible elements of their inhuman nature became apparent. Not only were they too pale, but all of them were covered by scattered patches of mold.

I noticed a hole in the leg of Ronald Willis's jeans. Only the hole went much deeper than that. It was a deep, ragged wound with burnt, jagged edges: I could see down through the layers of decayed skin and muscle, where the blackened femur was exposed.

I allowed myself a quick glance at the other two: They also bore wounds that would be enough to incapacitate if not kill a living person: There was a long vertical gash down the center of the dark-haired one's chest, revealing a yellowed sternum. The young man with the blondish red hair had an abdominal wound that was not only grisly to look at—it should have prevented him from getting out of that car, let alone walking toward me.

One of them had said that they had been about to "split". They had done a lot tonight, with the destruction of Jimmy Wilson's car. Maybe their power was partially spent. That certainly appeared to be the case. While the three apparitions standing beside the wrecked Mercury Montclair were formidable enough, they didn't look capable of overpowering a speeding car, and destroying it as Jimmy's car had been destroyed.

The one with the reddish blond hair looked at Leah.

"We gotta take the dolly, Ronny. Oh, man, it has been so long, you know?"

Leah screamed when she realized what they intended. Then she screamed again when a little swarm of four or five cockroaches scurried out of the reddish blond one's mouth, skittering across his face.

He paused to angrily wipe them away. I wondered: Was there enough memory left in him—enough residual humanity—for him to realize how disgusting he was?

But I had no time to pursue such speculations. Ronny was practically among the three of us. He reached out for Leah, and I saw that his hands were burned down to the finger bones.

I swung the ax at Ronald Willis, almost blindly. I had barely enough foresight to aim my blow at the last second. The blade connected squarely with one of his arms, and the momentum of the arc made the ax head pass cleanly through the arm. It fell to the pavement.

The next few seconds passed in a blur. The three apparitions were lunging for me, even as I was raising the ax again. But I realized that I didn't have the stomach to stand my ground and chop all of them to pieces. That simply wasn't in me.

So I turned to my two friends, first Leah and then Bobby, and said, *"Run!"*

I stood there for another split second to confirm that they had obeyed me.

Then I dropped the ax, allowing it to clatter to the road, and turned and ran myself.

18

T he three of us ran for perhaps half a mile. I trailed Leah and Bobby for about half of that, then they started to slow with fatigue, and eventually I caught up with them.

I didn't permit myself so much as a backward glance. I was all too certain that if I looked back, I would see Ronald Willis running, or even flying behind me, intent on avenging the loss of his burned, skeletal arm.

That didn't happen, though. When Leah and Bobby stopped running, I finally stopped myself, and it was then that I looked behind me: There was nothing in my wake but an empty street, and ordinary suburban houses on both sides. There were telephone poles and the large trees that characterized this older section of the neighborhood. There were cars parked silently in driveways, mailboxes, and the full moon overhead. But no sign of Ronald Willis, Larry Sturgis, or Jerry Ames.

"Are we safe now?" Leah asked, panting. "I mean—relatively speaking."

I was panting hard, too. I would discover track and cross country later, in high school; but in junior high I wasn't very athletic. I leaned over and rested my hands on my knees, breathing hard. Then I looked up and answered Leah.

"Relatively speaking, yes, I think. We caught a lucky break back there. You both saw what they did to Jimmy Wilson's car. That must have sapped most of their strength. They were—fading."

"Fading," Bobby replied reflectively. "If only Matt Stefano could 'fade', huh?"

I wasn't sure if Bobby intended this remark as a challenge (he knew that I was afraid of Matt Stefano) or simply as an offhand observation. (Bobby was more than a little afraid of Matt Stefano himself, for that matter.) At any rate, though, I wasn't in the mood for talking about Matt Stefano at the moment. We hadn't seen him for the better part of an hour. (We hadn't seen much of anyone for the better part of an hour.) I was willing to mentally set Matt Stefano aside until school resumed on Monday. I needed to set him aside. I could only worry about so many things at once.

"Yeah," I answered Bobby. "Something like that."

"Have you guys had trouble with Matt Stefano?" Leah asked.

"He's not exactly our friend," Bobby said.

"That's one way to put it," I agreed.

Leah paused for a moment, then shook her head dismissively. Luckily, she didn't seem interested in talking about Matt Stefano, or our troubles with him.

"So I guess we keep walking," she said at length.

"That's all that we can do."

We started walking again. No one seemed to feel like talking. This gave me a few much-needed minutes with my own thoughts, where I could ponder our situation. Several times now a cycle of events had repeated itself: We would appear to be in the clear, and then things would get worse again.

I would require many years of reflection to reach the conclusion that our Halloween walk was not unlike the broader walk of life itself: Salvation could come out of nowhere, but so could disaster. Similarly, self-determination was a very real force—but self-determination had its limits.

That night, through my own efforts, I had made genuine progress with Leah. I had overcome my fears and become a leader of my peers.

But at root I was still vulnerable. At the end of the day, I was nothing but a very mortal twelve-year-old boy, alone in a hostile universe.

"How long till we're home, do you think?" Leah asked, interrupting my thoughts.

"Maybe half an hour," I said. "If we make good time."

"Then let's make good time," Bobby said.

Those words caused us all to quicken our pace just a bit. Bobby, who occasionally smoked cigarettes, told us to slow down.

"I said make good time. I didn't say run."

Interesting: Bobby was taller than me, and would definitely have the advantage in a fight. He was braver when facing bullies like Matt Stefano. But he wasn't conventionally athletic.

"You need to quit smoking," Leah told him. Leah and I both knew about Bobby's cigarette habit, and neither of us approved. Most of the time, we left the issue alone; but once in a while we prodded him about it.

"Smoking doesn't hurt you," Bobby said. "That's all government propaganda. My old man said so, in fact. I'm not going to die of lung cancer."

Knowing Bobby's touchiness about anything concerning his father, I decided to leave that one alone. He was wrong about the government propaganda, I think. He was right about one thing, though: Bobby Nagel would not die of lung cancer.

Suddenly, Leah held up her hand, signaling Bobby and me to stop.

"Look," she said at a volume that was little more than a whisper. "Up there."

"I don't see anything," Bobby said in a normal voice.

Leah shushed him with a frantic wave of her hand.

"Up there," she repeated.

Then I saw it; and the gasp that escaped from Bobby's throat told me that he saw it, too.

We were walking down a long section of this residential street that formed a straightaway, so we had a clear view for perhaps half a mile in the moonlight, and with the ambient light given off by a smattering of the surrounding houses. The tall figure that was approaching us was silhouetted by this light.

"Step back from the road," I said. I reached out and pulled both Leah and Bobby back. Quietly, we moved into the adjacent yard, taking us out of the roadway.

The still approaching figure might have been seven or even eight feet tall, with broad shoulders and a roughly human shape.

I say "roughly human", because at least one anatomical feature suggested inhumanness—even in silhouette. The ears on either side of the figure's head were so long that they stood out distinctly. These were ears that belonged on a wolf or a jackal, perhaps, but not a man.

The mystery didn't end there. The figure was carrying what looked to be a sack, slung over one shoulder. In his free hand, he was carrying a long, tapered object. We could still see only his shape, but the contours of the object were clear enough: He was carrying a long machete. *A chopping knife*, I thought, not yet grasping the prescience of my observation.

We as yet had no idea what this thing—this creature—might be. One thing was certain, though: It would not be friendly.

"We've got to hide!" I said.

Bobby and Leah both looked at me as I made this painfully obvious statement. Of course we had to hide. In desperation, all three of us made a quick scan of our surroundings. We were in a residential front yard that was mostly barren but for a single oak tree that could not possibly hide the three of us. There was no car in the driveway.

"Okay, so where do we hide?" Bobby asked.

I looked across the street: there was a large hedge in the opposite yard that looked promising.

"We can't go over there," Leah said, as if reading my thoughts. "He —it's—too close. He'll see us."

Leah was right; the figure with the sack and the machete was drawing down upon us. So far, the thing did not appear to be aware of us. That would change in less than a minute if we didn't take cover.

Then there was a clicking sound, and the unmistakable creak of hinges. We all turned around, toward the house nearest us.

The old man standing in the doorway of the house was older—in his sixties or seventies. He was no taller than Bobby, and of slight build. A shock of white hair covered his head.

He beckoned to us: *"Come on!"* he said, in a voice that was just loud enough for us to hear. The old man gestured in the direction of the approaching figure. *"There isn't much time!"*

For all any of us knew, this old man could be another vampire, or ghost, or something even worse. But we had a stark choice to make: We either trusted him, or we took our chances with the figure coming down the street.

"I say we trust him," Leah said, speaking for all of us.

"I agree," I said.

Bobby nodded his agreement.

"Come on!" the old man said, a little louder this time, and with great urgency. "Or the head collector will see you!"

We didn't need any further encouragement. We ran for the front door of the little house, exercising the minimal caution needed to leap over the step of the front porch without tripping. A chance injury, I reminded myself again, would be very, very inconvenient tonight.

The old man stepped back and ushered us inside, quickly and in single file.

Head collector? I thought as the old man closed the door behind us.

We were all taken aback by the interior of the house—not because of anything unusual, but because of the exact opposite. We had spent the past two hours, more or less, lost in a world that was quite apart from our normal, everyday existence. A world where nothing could be assumed and nothing could be trusted.

The interior of this house was lit with soft warm light. It was filled with oak furniture, and the floor of the living room was covered with light hardwood and deep blue throw rugs. Every available surface—the end tables, the mantelshelf above the fireplace, and the coffee table—was covered with either doilies or knickknacks, or both. The house was cluttered but neat, and a little too warm—as is common with the homes of the elderly.

All of this decorating suggested a feminine touch. Above the mantelshelf was a portrait of a young man in a navy dress uniform with a pretty young woman in a bridal dress and veil. I could tell that it was from the World War II era, both from the woman's hairstyle, and the sepia, halftone appearance of the color. I looked quickly to the old man's face and saw an immediate resemblance, despite the elapsed decades. This man and his wife, then, a long, long time ago.

"My name is George," the old man said. "And you're lucky that I happened to be on the alert tonight. I had an odd feeling about this Halloween night. Did any of you see Albert? He looks to be about fifteen or so, but he's really—well, he's really a ghost."

We all nodded. I gave George a brief account of our interactions with the ghost boy, describing both him and his usual attire.

"In my day," George said, "he wore bib overalls and he went by the name of Albert. But I think we're talking about the same entity."

"You—you saw him, too?" Leah asked, amazed.

"Uh-huh—the year I turned thirteen. Let me guess: You kids are probably about thirteen, too. Am I right?"

"You're off by one year," Bobby said. "We're twelve."

George nodded. "Doesn't surprise me. Kids are growing up faster nowadays. Yes, I saw Albert—or the ghost boy—that year, in the weeks before Halloween. And on Halloween itself, I had to endure the trial—the 'twelve hours of testing'. I lived around here, you know. This subdivision wasn't built yet then, of course; but my parents had a little farm up the way. That was during the Great Depression. Hard Times.

"But that's another topic. What you saw outside there just now was something far worse than Albert the ghost boy. That thing was the head collector. I'm sure you saw that sack that he was carrying over his shoulder, right? Well, that sack was full of heads. And if you saw the sack, then you probably saw the big knife as well. I don't have to tell you what he does with that."

"Wait a minute," Bobby said, ever the skeptical one. "You mean to tell us that that thing—the 'head collector'—is going around chopping people's heads off?"

"That's one way of putting it," George affirmed.

"Then I suppose that tomorrow there will be a big news story about all the missing people from around here—all the ones without their heads?"

Bobby's skepticism was not lost on George. But the old man had nothing to prove to this adolescent boy, and he responded patiently.

"If you want to understand this, my young friend, then you need to think 'outside the box'. Yes, the head collector chops off heads. But he makes a long journey between places on Halloween night. Some of those heads in his sack might be from California, or India, or Mexico. And some of them might have been taken tonight, and some of them might have been taken fifty or a hundred years ago. If you've been observant tonight, then you've probably noticed that time does curious things on Halloween nights like this one. Did any of you see the young girl, Elmira?"

"Yes." I told George about our encounter with Elmira. Then Leah chimed in and told him about how I had opened the gate for her.

"I'm glad you did that," George said. "She asked me to help her, but I was afraid." George clapped me gently on the shoulder. "You're a brave young man. Anyway, you probably also noticed that Elmira is not from this time of ours; she was very, very old even when I was a boy in the 1930s—even though she looked very much like a normal little girl, except for..."

"Yes," I said. George was obviously referring to the horrible injury on one side of her head. The blow from the Shawnee tomahawk that had killed her. "Except for that."

It occurred to me then that although we were inside this man's house, we hadn't yet introduced ourselves.

"I'm Jeff Schaeffer," I said, extending a hand. "This is Leah Carter and Bobby Nagel."

Each of us shook hands with George, and the scene, once again, struck me with its civility and normality, after everything that we had been through.

"Your wife keeps a nice house," Leah said. She had noticed the photo above the mantelpiece, too, and she had made the connection.

"My wife passed away almost ten years ago," George said. "No—that's all right; you couldn't have known, could you?"

George must have seen Leah staring at the picture. "Yes, that's us, we were married in Norfolk, Virginia, in 1944. I was in the navy then, as you can probably tell. I had just spent a year dodging German U-boats in the North Atlantic. My overseas duty was finally over."

Bobby signaled to another photograph, enclosed within a standup frame atop George's old Zenith television set, that I had not yet noticed. It was another young man in a military uniform. He was in his early twenties and he looked vaguely like George—also a bit like the woman who was with George in the portrait above the mantelpiece. There was a U.S. flag behind the young man. This photo did not appear to be recent, but it was not nearly as old as the portrait above the fireplace.

"Is that your son?" Bobby asked.

"Yes," George said. "That was my son. He was killed in Vietnam in 1968. Have you ever heard of the Tet Offensive?"

We all shook our heads. I thought that I might have heard the term somewhere, but there was no way I could possibly explain it. Obviously it had been some incident or phase of the Vietnam War.

"We were all born in 1968," Bobby said. "We don't remember."

"No," George said. "I suppose you wouldn't. It was at the end of January of that year. My son was stationed just outside Saigon. He was in aviation mechanics. He worked on the big helicopters. His location was overrun—during the offensive."

I felt—and I'm sure that Bobby and Leah must have felt—that we should have been able to offer some useful and meaningful reflection. But we were three adolescents who were as yet inexperienced with death, as all but the unluckiest adolescents tend to be.

And as for Vietnam, we knew next to nothing about it. My father was in the military—but his service ended right before Vietnam started heating up. While Leah's father had been of military age at that time, he had done his service stateside, in the Ohio National Guard. Bobby's father had been a peace protestor, and my parents sometimes quipped that Bobby's old man was still living the hippy lifestyle.

George sighed. Remembering the death of his son seemed to arouse in him a sadness that eclipsed the sadness felt over the loss of his wife. This made sense, according to a certain logic: George's wife had lived a fairly long life, at least into her late middle age years. George's son, meanwhile, had been cut down in his youth, before he'd even reached his prime.

There was a sadness in this solitary household, normal and welcoming though it was. George was a man living alone with little more than the memories of those he had loved. I wanted to comfort him, wanted my two friends to comfort him. But I also sensed that there was little we could do for George. We were not the ones he wanted, after all. He was being kind to us because we were three kids in a jam. Also, like Jimmy, George had some past experience with many of the things we had seen this night.

I therefore did not try to comfort him—an effort which I knew would be futile, anyway. Instead I asked for his advice.

"What do you think we should do, George?" (I was not accustomed to calling unfamiliar adults by their first names; but George was the only name he had given us. And besides, these circumstances permitted a breakdown of the normal formalities.)

But George had no immediate, pithy advice to offer. *(So much for the fallback strategy of relying on adults for wisdom.)* In fact, he seemed to be almost as confused as we were.

"It's strange," George said. "I haven't seen the head collector in years. His appearance isn't a very common occurrence, you know. I noticed that there weren't any trick-or-treaters, which is fairly unusual for this street. I therefore suspected that something was up. I walked outside and, sure enough, I saw him coming...And then I saw the three of you."

"Does the head collector know we're here?"

As if in answer to my question, there was a loud pounding at the front door. It rattled the doorframe, and seemed to rattle the entire front end of the house as well.

"Quiet!" George said in a low whisper. He held a finger up to his lips. The finger was noticeably shaking. "He'll go away. Hopefully."

After waiting perhaps a full minute, George spoke again, still in a whisper. "Strange. I haven't seen him for years. And he hasn't actually bothered me since I was a boy. It must be because—"

Then George caught himself and stopped, though I knew exactly what he had been about to say. The head collector had come to George's door because the three of us were here. George had interfered with the cycle of the curse by offering us refuge. He had intervened.

"I'll protect you," George said—because that was what any decent adult would do under the circumstances.

I realized, though, on some level, that George would not be able to protect us from the thing that had pounded on that door. Not for long, anyway.

"We can't stay here," I said. Bobby and Leah both gawped at me, horrified.

There was a loud, rumbling growl that gave me a sudden chill and put an immediate end to all conversation. From where we stood in George's living room, we had a clear view of the picture window at the rear of the dining room. The glass door was covered with a flimsy curtain; but the light of the full moon and George's rear floodlights cast a horrifying shadow: It was the head collector. The shadow was distinct enough to allow us to make out his sack and his long beheading knife. There was no doubt concerning his presence.

A scratching sound against the glass. The message was clear. If we didn't come out, the head collector would come in to get us. It was only a matter of time.

The shadow moved away. We all knew that it would be back.

"That was a message," I said, addressing Bobby and Leah. "If we don't go, then that thing will come in and get us. Inside the house, we'll be cornered and killed. We won't have a chance. And—" I turned to our host—"George will be killed, too. Our only real chance is to run."

"Are you saying you want to go out there with that thing?" Leah asked.

"No, I don't *want* to. I'm saying that's our only choice."

"Jeff is right," Bobby said. "He'll come through that glass like nothing. It's a wonder he hasn't already."

In the intervening years since that night, I have often pondered the very question that Bobby had just proposed. The head collector could have, of course, come immediately through the glass door in George's dining room.

Perhaps the curse had its own set of rules and limitations, though, for both sides. The entities that were part of this thing were powerful, but they weren't omnipotent. Nor did they have complete and total carte blanche to go anywhere, to attack anyone. The curse had originally fallen on my head. Then Bobby and Leah had involved themselves through their association with me. Jimmy Wilson had gotten too close to us at the wrong time and place, where the boundaries between the worlds happened to be dangerously thin.

And now George had involved himself, too: Originally he had been drawn in because of his unusual perception—owing to his childhood experiences. Then he had made himself our protector.

His house might still be technically off-limits to the head collector. But that would change if he sheltered us for too long.

I looked back at George: "Do you have any ideas as to how we might get out of here without getting killed by that thing?"

George paused to ponder the question. All of us—myself included—were anticipating the head collector's violent entry into the house at any moment.

"Well," George finally said, "the head collector is very, very slow—or at least that's what I remember."

"He seemed to be walking at a pretty good clip," Bobby said.

"What I mean," George clarified, "is that he's not very smart. It isn't very difficult to confuse him. We could use that to our advantage."

"How so?"

"I have an idea," George said. "I'll open the back door—not the big glass door in the dining room, but the one in the kitchen. I'll distract him. Then you can run."

Leah shook her head dubiously. George's plan could be dissected and found to be flawed from any number of angles. We didn't have time for a lengthy debate, though.

I felt that I should make a counterproposal—something that wouldn't expose the old man to such obvious risk. George's plan was risky for us, too.

But my mind drew a blank.

"Okay," I said at length. "I guess that would work."

"I don't know," Leah said.

"None of us knows," Bobby said. "That's the point. But we have to do *something*. We can't stay here."

"All right," George said. "Let's do it before we change our minds." The old man turned abruptly. He passed through his dining room. We heard his footsteps on the linoleum of the kitchen floor.

"I'm going to open the back door now!" he called out. "I'll distract the head collector. Then the three of you can run out the front door. I'll tell you when I see him. I'll tell you when to go. Wait for my signal. Oh—and don't forget to lock the door behind you, please. An open door—well, I believe that might be perceived as an invitation. The rules, you know."

The rules? The old man had just confirmed what I had suspected throughout the night: that tonight's paranormal activity was governed by a set of rules which were, to some extent, both fixed and knowable. I wished that I had more time with George—more time to pick his brain for information.

But there was no time.

"Come on," I said. I placed my hand on the front door knob and waited for George's signal.

I heard George open the back door with a series of clicks and creaking hinges. I heard him call out:

"Hey, head collector! Where are you? Get any heads tonight?"

"Go!" I shouted to my friends. I pulled the front door open, and Leah and Bobby rushed out behind me, the latter practically knocking me down. In a matter of seconds we were out in the night air again, beyond whatever degree of protection George's house had provided us.

"Close the door!" I shouted. I whirled around in time to see Bobby pull the door shut behind him.

"Now run! Run like hell!"

Running through the front yard, we made it halfway down to the road when the head collector stepped out from behind a tree.

The head collector was indeed seven or eight feet tall, and broad across the shoulders. The tree, another old pin oak, hadn't fully concealed his bulk. But we had been too infused with adrenalin to notice him.

Time seemed to freeze as I took in additional details: The head collector's features had some human characteristics, but they were fused with something else—or perhaps several other things. He had an elongated mouth that no human had, and yellow eyes. His entire body was covered in a short, dark, bristly-looking fur. The head collector wasn't naked: he was wearing a crude pair of trousers and the torn remnants of a now colorless shirt.

Now I realized my mistake—the mistake that might mean the deaths of all three of us: I had told Bobby and Leah to bolt as soon as I heard George open the rear door and call for the head collector. But George had told me to wait for a specific signal from him. George had had no time to actually distract the head collector, which had been the old man's plan.

The plan, however good or bad it might have been, was all for naught now. I was going to die. Leah and Bobby were going to die.

And it would be all my fault.

The head collector dropped his sack. To my horror, it was indeed filled with heads, and several of them rolled out. The face of a pale-skinned man stared blankly up at us, his still open eyes reflecting the terror of his last seconds of life. Another head, with brown skin and black hair, might have indeed been from India. I also saw the head of a young woman; her blonde ponytail had been severed along with her neck.

The head collector raised his machete. Its improbably long blade was stained with the blood of previous beheadings.

He was going to take our heads, one by one.

This was it; this was the end. I had managed to live not quite thirteen years so far, only to die in George's front yard. My parents would never even know what had happened to me, in all likelihood.

Then suddenly, I heard George call out.

"Hey you! Why don't you pick on someone your own size?"

George was standing off to the left of us, in the narrow strip of lawn that separated the front yard from the back yard. The old man was visibly shaking, but he was doing his utmost to project an air of defiant, taunting arrogance.

"Whatsamatter, head collector? You afraid of a little old man? Why don't you pick on someone your own size?"

George's dare had an aspect of absurdity, of course. He was only slightly taller than Bobby and me, and probably no heavier than Bobby. Moreover, he was a somewhat frail elderly man. And the head collector was huge—larger than any man I had ever seen.

The head collector, without lowering his knife, looked toward George and bared his teeth.

"Yeah, you recognize me, don't you? You and I have tangled before, haven't we?" George taunted. George had told us that he had endured the curse as a young boy and encountered the head collector. He had been short on details. This taunt suggested that George—a daring old man by any estimate—had been an even more daring boy.

The head collector paused for a moment. Leah, Bobby, and I began to slowly back up. From our present position, the head collector could lunge laterally and slash any one of us with his machete if we tried to make a run for it. If we managed to back up a few more paces, though, we would be able to outflank him and escape.

"You missed me back then!" George shouted. "Bet you can't get me now!"

The head collector abruptly turned away from Leah, Bobby and me and began walking at a steady pace toward George. *Run!* I wanted to shout at the old man. Although the head collector did not appear to walk faster than the average well-conditioned man, his enormous height gave him a large stride.

I motioned to my two friends. *"Come on!"* I waved them forward and we all began running again.

George probably intended that we would keep running without looking back. None of us could do that, though. We stopped when we reached the road and turned around.

George had begun to flee the head collector, as he had presumably fled him all those years ago. But he was now a half-century older, and much slower. We all watched in abject horror as George stopped and grabbed his chest. Whether the problem was his heart—or simply a shortness of breath—we did not know and would never know.

George whirled around at the last second. His legs were frozen beneath him, useless for all practical purposes. The head collector, meanwhile, resumed his unhurried but deliberate steps. He closed on George with the machete raised high above his head.

No! This can't be happening. This won't *happen!* I thought, my mind now a swirl of total panic, even though I was relatively safe for the moment in my position on the road.

The machete came down in a wide, swift arc and connected with George's neck before he could even raise a hand to deflect the blow (not that this would have been likely to help him much). The machete, driven by the strength of the head collector's muscled and hair-covered arm, sliced cleanly through George's neck with a wet, cracking sound.

George's head rolled off his shoulders and fell into the grass of his lawn. His body buckled at the knees and waist and fell forward.

I heard Leah scream beside me, though I'm not sure if she was the only one who screamed. If I didn't scream, I certainly felt like it.

The head collector bent and picked up George's severed head. It was still dripping blood. He carried it like a football to where he had dropped his sack. He lifted the bag by one side and he irreverently tossed his grisly prize inside. Reaching down, he lifted the two or three heads that had earlier tumbled out. His hands were so large that he could lift each head by grasping it with a single open palm, like a person would grasp a cantaloupe.

"We've got to get out of here!" I said to Leah and Bobby. I wanted to stay and pay my respects to George in some way; and I imagined that this was what they were probably thinking. There was nothing we could do for George now, though. We could only stay here where the head collector would catch us, too; and the old man's death would be entirely in vain.

"I can't go," Leah said. She was watching the head collector gather his trophies with a nearly catatonic expression on her face. I suspected that she was beginning to go into shock. I was close to shock myself.

God, help me. Please!

I had never really prayed very much before. Not that I was an atheist or anything. I went to Catholic school, and I had already sat through what seemed like hundreds or thousands of church services. If asked, I would have answered that I believed in God. But who really needs God at the age of twelve?

"You can go, Leah!" I said. "You *have* to go! If you don't move, you're going to die. We're all going to die. *Now move!*"

I tugged her arm, and she ran when I ran. Bobby followed. We had not begun our flight a second too soon. The head collector, having added George's head to his nightly total, was eagerly intent on adding three more.

19

Wе had no idea where we were running to. Although all of us had been through this section of the Shayton Estates neighborhood at one time or another, none of us was really familiar with it.

Two houses down from George's (and on the opposite side of the street) we swerved into a yard. It was a random move, really. We were acutely aware of the head collector following behind us. He was carrying his knife and his bag, not running fast, but walking quickly with his long strides and tireless determination.

The side of this particular yard was shielded from view by a row of pine trees. It was just possible, I thought, that the cover provided by these trees would prevent the head collector from seeing us and tracking our progress. I was soon to be proven wrong in this regard.

We ran through the side yard and into the back yard. Our plan (not that we actually had one) would have been to cut through this back yard into the back yard that abutted this one. This course of action would have given us many chances to weave among trees and houses, hopefully losing the head collector in the process.

But when we reached the rear of the back yard, we came to a high chain link fence. The fence separated the yard from a sloping wooded hillside that abutted a two-lane highway called Clough Pike.

Bobby ran up to the fence and grasped with both hands the links that made the diamond-patterned lattice. He stared down the hillside. We all stared. Then he looked up at the top of the fence, which was easily two feet taller than any of us.

"Can we make it?" Bobby asked.

My mind was so tired now. I was only twelve. I wasn't equipped to make decisions like this under pressure.

But what had I told Leah? I had told her, more or less, that you do what you have to do. You do what needs to be done.

"Impossible," I said. "First of all, we can't get over it."

"I could get up there if you boosted me."

"But then who would boost me? Leah? Sorry, Leah—but I don't think you're strong enough. And then who would boost Leah, with you and I on the other side of the fence?"

Bobby snorted. "Damn it!"

"And besides," I went on. "Look at that hillside. Even if you could get over the fence, you wouldn't be able to control your landing."

The contour of the hillside was largely visible in the moonlight: The drop-off on the other side of the fence was steep; and the hillside was dotted with fallen branches, rocks, and jagged stumps.

"All right then, so what do we do?"

One option was to run back to the road. That was too risky now, though. If we went back to the road, we would run right into the path of the head collector.

I looked around the immediate vicinity of the (dark) house and the back yard. Then I saw something that gave me an idea: One window on the side of the house was partially ajar. The window was about shoulder-high. Based on its location, it would provide a passage into the garage.

And the window would be too small for the head collector to enter.

It wasn't a perfect plan, but it was the only plan we had, and the seconds were ticking down against us. I quickly communicated my idea to Bobby and Leah.

"Not bad, Schaeffer," Bobby said. "But not very good, either."

"I don't think *very* good is possible right now."

"Come on, you guys," Leah said. "That...*thing* will be here any second."

We hustled over to the partially ajar window. The homeowner had probably left it open during the previous weekend, when temperatures had briefly soared into the upper seventies—uncharacteristically warm for late October in Ohio.

I placed my hands on the lower sash of the window and pushed upwards. To my relief, the window slid easily. I stole a brief glance inside the garage: Amid the shadows I could make out the shapes of a workbench on the opposite wall, metal shelving, an empty gasoline can, paint cans, and a coiled garden hose.

"Bobby," I said, "you go in first. Then I'll help Leah in and you can help her down from the other side."

"Then we'll run into the same problem we ran into back at that fence," Bobby protested. "Who will help you up? You'll be the last person?"

"I'll manage," I said. "Hurry!"

I looked back over my shoulder and scanned the yard of this house and the neighboring one, then the roadway. There was no sign of the head collector yet. We had gotten a good lead on him, weighed down as he was with his sack full of severed heads. But he would be tracking us. There wasn't much time.

I bent my knees slightly and made a stirrup with my interlaced hands. Bobby placed one foot in my joined palms, while he simultaneously gripped the window sill. I boosted him up, straining beneath his weight, while making sure that I didn't propel him headfirst into the upper sash of the window.

We caught another lucky break. The opening of the window was more than wide enough for Bobby to fit through it. Since Bobby was the largest of us, that meant that both Leah and I would fit easily.

Bobby's foot shifted out of my hand and swung within a few inches of my face. His torso was entirely inside the garage now. Bobby wriggled the rest of the way inside, with a few grunts and deep breaths. His feet disappeared inside the window.

There was the sound of a crash as Bobby fell into the garage. For a few seconds his situation was uncertain. Then he stood up, still smarting from the fall, and said: "It's okay. There are half a dozen bundles of old newspaper just beneath the window. Not exactly a mattress, but it broke my fall. Leah, I'll help you inside from this end, and you shouldn't fall at all."

"Leah, your turn," I said. I repeated the maneuver with Leah, bending my knees and making a foothold. It was much easier to boost Leah, as she was much, much lighter. Bobby, as promised, helped her gently descend through the open window space to the inside of the garage.

I was now the only one standing outside in the yard. I looked through the window and saw Leah and Bobby, who were safely inside —or at least relatively safe.

I looked over my shoulder once more. No sign of the head collector.

"Don't waste time looking back," Bobby said. "You've got to move, Schaeffer. Give me your hand."

Bobby was right; there was no time to waste. I reached inside the open window and Bobby clasped my hand.

"Now walk yourself up the wall. I'll pull you in from this side."

I did as he instructed. I placed my right foot against the brick exterior of the house, as Bobby tugged on my arm. With my free hand I grabbed the windowsill.

I was poised against the exterior wall of the house somewhat like a mountain climber, with one foot still in the grass. I lifted my left foot off the ground, with the intention of cantilevering myself into the window, with Bobby's help, of course.

But instead I fell backward. Bobby swore loudly as my hand slipped from his grasp. As I fell back, both feet touched the earth, and I tried to at least regain my balance. Instead I was driven backward by my own momentum. I took a hard pratfall in the yard.

I sat there on the lawn for a few seconds, seeing stars, my butt smarting. The temperature had fallen since we had left a few hours ago, and the ground was both cold and unexpectedly damp.

"Schaeffer!" I heard Bobby say, "you've got to get u—"

That was when I heard the sound of an inhuman snort, and heavy footsteps. I whirled around from my seated position, and saw the head collector trudging through the front yard of this house. His sack was slung over one shoulder, his large machete dangled from the opposite hand.

I had no way of knowing if the head collector was aware of my presence or not. In either case, another attempt at the garage window was out of the question. The head collector would surely see me, and he could pluck me down at his leisure. He would also see Leah and Bobby in their hiding place.

I turned briefly to Bobby, who was still standing in the open window. I waved to him frantically. I held my finger to my lips, signaling him to be silent. Then I waved him away from the window.

I looked around for some immediate cover: My only option was a patch of shrubbery and rose bushes beneath the window to one side. The shrubs and bushes were all brown and skeletal. But they were all I had.

I scooted myself along the ground and pushed my back up against the wall. Clods of dried mud and landscaping bark dug into my pants.

On the side of me nearest to the head collector, there was a large shrub. In between me and the shrub was a small rosebush. I noticed that the rose bush was secured in place with a stake that protruded about a foot out of the ground. The submerged end of the stake, I reasoned, should be sharp. Using one hand, trying to be silent and inconspicuous, I worked the stake free from the soil.

My efforts to be inconspicuous were completely in vain. I had barely removed the stake from the ground and laid it beside me when the head collector's shadow fell across the moonlit patch of lawn directly in front of me.

There would be no possibility of escape this time. George had given his life to help me escape the previous time I'd been face-to-face with the head collector. George was now dead, though, and there would be no one to take his place.

The head collector stared down at me with his yellow eyes. He dropped his sack on the ground. The sole mercy of this moment was that the bag did not spill open again. Even as my own death neared, I could not avoid the realization that poor George's head would be inside that bag.

The head collector smiled at me. Yes—I might have been projecting, imagining the expression; but I'm almost sure of it. The head collector was sizing me up with an evil satisfaction that was almost—*almost*—human.

The head collector's smile revealed two rows of sharp teeth. I thought again of the witch: Did everything in this horrible parallel world have such wicked-looking teeth?

Then he said something to me. I couldn't make out the words. They were words in a language that, I am certain, no human being has spoken for thousands of years, if humans ever spoke such a language at all. The head collector was telling me that he was going to kill me now—that there was nothing for me to do but reconcile myself to the inevitable.

I looked down at the wooden stake beside me in the dirt, the one that only minutes ago had been affixed to the dried out rosebush. I noted the tapered end of the stake.

Not pausing to think—moving with all the quickness I could possibly muster—I picked up the stake and rammed the sharp end of it into the head collector's nearest shin. This did little real damage, but it caused the head collector to raise that foot in a reflex action. His feet were bare, I now noted for the first time. His feet, though humanoid, were wide, and long, and covered with the same bristly fur that covered the rest of his body.

The head collector's left foot was poised directly above my head for a brief instant. I struck again with the tip of the stake. This time I rammed the point into the sole of his foot. I simultaneously grasped the shaft of the stake with my other hand, and pushed upward with all my might, even as the head collector pushed down—for he was off balance and had no choice but to lower his foot.

I rolled out of the way as the head collector pitched forward, already bellowing in rage and pain. He collapsed onto his knees, then fell backward again.

The wooden stake had passed through his foot. His impaled foot was now halfway between both ends of the stake.

The head collector's back slammed down on the lawn. He opened his lupine mouth and howled. His head tossed from side to side.

I pushed myself further away from him. He saw me, and made a short-lived effort to stand. The stake prevented that: it prevented him from standing up, and the agony of the injury was obviously excruciating.

Good, I thought bitterly, ever mindful of what the head collector had done to George.

I stood there watching him, saying nothing, while he watched me and howled. We stared each other down like that for perhaps a full minute.

I heard the mechanical sound of the house's automatic garage door being raised. Bobby and Leah emerged from the garage. They looked at the head collector on the ground (both maintaining a safe distance) then looked at me.

"How did you manage that one, Schaeffer?" Bobby asked. "We heard that thing screaming, so we figured you must have hurt it somehow, but—"

"A long story," I told him. "I got in a lucky blow."

"A lot of lucky blows for you tonight, huh?" He smiled.

The head collector's machete lay on the lawn not far from him, but far enough away that he could not possibly reach it. The blade glinted in the moonlight, and its surface was slick with blood.

George's blood.

If I were so inclined, I would be able to retrieve the machete, and lop the head collector's own head off. That would complete the David-and-Goliath metaphor, wouldn't it? That would bring things to a state of closure.

I knew, deep down, that I would be perfectly justified in finishing him off this way, and a part of me felt that this was exactly what I should do.

Then I pictured myself actually doing it, imagined fully what it would be like to swing that large blade, and cut through the fur, muscle and bone that held the head collector's head attached to his shoulders.

David had been up to such a task in the Old Testament, but I knew at that instant that I was no David. I was Jeff Schaeffer. I was only twelve, and I had known precious little of real violence. Justified as a deathblow might be, I was incapable of administering it.

"Let's go," I said to Bobby and Leah. "I don't think he'll bother us anymore."

Neither one of them was anxious to hang around there. The sack full of heads was emitting a noxious odor, we now realized. It was impossible to stand so close to it without contemplating the objects inside.

We were walking down the road when Jeff clapped me on the shoulder, looked at me, and looked back at the thrashing, supine figure of the head collector. He, or it—or whatever the head collector was—the creature was still howling with rage.

"I'll be damned," Bobby said. "You beat that thing, Schaeffer. And don't try to tell me otherwise. You really did beat it."

20

As we put more distance between ourselves and the head collector, the sound of his screams faded. Eventually we reached the point where we couldn't hear him at all.

Nevertheless, none of us really felt like talking. Too much had happened tonight. It was odd; I could recall few long silences when I was with Bobby or Leah (let alone both of them). But things had changed tonight, hadn't they? Unbeknownst to me at that moment, they were going to change more, even though Halloween was almost over.

"Not far to go," I told them. I don't know if I said this for my sake or theirs. I figured they could use some encouragement. Heck—I could have used some encouragement. As had been the pattern throughout the evening, I was coming down from the high of an adrenalin rush, entering a foggy territory that felt like it might be the beginnings of clinical shock.

"We'll be home soon," I added. This was true, wasn't it? It had to be true.

"What if home is gone?" Leah asked. "I mean—what if we arrive home, and our homes have become these horrible places?

Bobby looked awkwardly away. Even under normal circumstances, his home life was far less ideal than Leah's and mine were.

"That won't happen," I told Leah—even though the same question weighed on my mind. "We have to have—" I paused, not sure of the concept I was trying to express.

"Faith?" Leah supplied. "Is that the word you're looking for?"

It hadn't been, really; but it seemed to fit. "Yeah, I guess so."

Yes, we had to have faith that when we returned home, things would be just as they had been before. We would each go back to our individual, familiar versions of reality.

That faith—or *belief*, if you prefer—would mean something very different to Bobby from what it would mean to either Leah or me. So just as we each had to have faith, we also had to decide what we could safely believe in. Every day, throughout our short lives, there had always been a distinct and unique reality waiting for each of us. Even if the curse completely lifted, that disparity and that uncertainty would still divide us. As I pondered that fact, it occurred to me that each one of us was very much alone, no matter how much time we might spend together.

"I'm still sad about George," Leah said. "He—he gave his life for us, you know?" She looked first at me, then at Bobby for confirmation.

"Yeah, I guess he did," Bobby said. "But he seemed to know what he was doing."

Bobby was right. There had been something about George's act of self-sacrifice that was knowing and deliberate. He hadn't simply been someone who was in the wrong place at the wrong time. First George had chosen to hail us and offer us shelter. Then he had chosen to walk around the side of his house and face the head collector, after we had run into the creature's path.

After I had jumped the gun, having neglected to wait for George's signal to run.

This was a line of thought that I did not dare explore too much at the moment. Don't get me wrong—I did feel guilty. But I also knew (in a way that I would not be able to articulate until many years of reflection had passed) that I had been thrust into a situation that was far beyond my years. How many kids my age had ever been faced with truly life-and-death decisions? Not very many, I would have guessed.

"What George did," I told Leah, "he did it with—full understanding. Do you know what I mean?"

At first Leah shook her head. Then she nodded, grasping my meaning. She started crying again.

Bobby, uncertain of how to handle the crying Leah, looked away. He quickened his pace just a bit, so that he pulled a little ahead of us.

"We're almost home," I told her. "We turn right on the next street, Benjamin Avenue. Then the next street will take us to the ones we live on."

I allowed myself a moment to savor that word, *home*. I pictured my mom and my dad, and my little sister, Carrie. Had my dad arrived home in time to take her out? Or was she still waiting for him in the kitchen?

Leah continued to look glum, the tears still in her eyes. With Bobby walking up ahead, I reached down and interlaced my hand in hers.

"It will be all right, Leah."

"Yes, but that poor old man."

I felt guilty for what I was about to do next. But I could do nothing to bring George back—even though my mistake had contributed to his death. He had made his own choice, I told myself. The old man had known exactly what he was doing.

I leaned toward Leah, and we both stopped while I kissed her. What was this? The third time this night? I broke the kiss and we continued walking. Bobby saw us. He shook his head, but he was smiling—perhaps glad for us, and perhaps merely resigned. If Bobby had ever thought that he was going to be the one to get Leah, that thought was dispelled now, wasn't it?

We walked a while more like that, Leah and I holding hands, and Bobby maintaining a respectful distance ahead of us. Then we all

heard a male voice shouting frantically—and I remembered that this
was a cursed night.

"Help! Help, you guys!"

It was easy enough to locate the source of the voice, but somewhat more difficult to process the situation before us: Matt Stefano
was standing behind a woodpile in the back yard of the property
directly adjacent to us. The woodpile was long and methodically
stacked about four feet high, so that it resembled a hedgerow.

The house to which the woodpile belonged was dark; and I
noticed that all of the nearby houses seemed to be dark. Were we
back in some sort of a twilight zone again, or were these simply the
homes of people who had gone out for the evening? There was no
way to tell.

Matt called out again:

"You guys gotta help me! I can't get out of here! I'm scared!"

I looked at Bobby. I had supplied most of the answers tonight,
when we were confronting supernatural threats. Matt Stefano fell
within Bobby's bailiwick.

"Forget it," Bobby said. "He's trying to trick us. This is an ambush
of some sort."

Matt could not possibly have heard Bobby's assessment, but he
seemed to sense the doubt.

"I'm not kidding, you guys! It's got me!"

"What's got you, Matt?" Bobby called out.

"I—I don't know what it is!" Matt answered. He looked downward,
in the direction of his feet—which were obscured from our view by
the woodpile. We could only see Matt from the chest up.

"Then I'm sure it's nothing you can't handle," Bobby countered.

"Nagel, I'm not joking around! This thing has got me!"

Bobby rolled his eyes and turned to me. "He's bullshitting us."

I tentatively nodded, but I wasn't sure: There were strange things
afoot tonight, and many of them were dangerous. Would it be so
unlikely for Matt to have encountered one of the night's multiple
hazards?

And what if he was telling the truth?

I had already contributed to the death of one innocent person tonight. True, Matt Stefano was not innocent in the same way that George had been innocent; but did he deserve to be left there, abandoned to something that might do him grave harm—possibly even kill him?

"We can't just leave him here," I said to Bobby. "What if he's really hurt?"

Bobby groaned. He pointed his finger at my chest. "I'm telling you, Schaeffer, I know that asshole, and I've got a real feeling about this. Matt Stefano is crying wolf. He wants us to come back there so he can spring some kind of a trap on us. There might even be two or three of his friends back there, ready to jump out from behind that woodpile and pound the tar out of you. And besides—what has Matt Stefano ever done for you? Do you think he'd help you out if you were in a jam?"

Bobby's logic was flawless, of course, within the context of everyday schoolyard morality. Matt Stefano was a jerk, a bully, and he shouldn't be trusted. Any and all contact with him was to be avoided whenever possible.

However, these weren't ordinary circumstances. This might be a matter of life and death.

Matt called out for help again, and I began to see the presence of my tormentor in a completely different light. Perhaps this was an opportunity in disguise, a chance to cap this horrible night with an act of forgiveness and reconciliation. Perhaps Matt Stefano would receive his own brand of redemption in the process. Matt would henceforth consider himself to be in my debt, and the two of us would become good friends after this, bully and victim no more.

Or—I could simply listen to Bobby and leave him back there.

"I'm going," I said finally.

"Schaeffer, don't!" Bobby said urgently. "Just keep walking. Like you said, we're almost done. We're practically home free."

"I—I've got to do this," I said, turning away from Bobby. He grabbed my arm but I shrugged him off.

"You do this, against my advice, and you're on your own."

"Whatever you say."

I began my walk toward the woodpile, where Matt Stefano was now watching me with great interest. He watched me as I approached. When I was about halfway there, he looked down at his feet again.

"Thank you, Schaeffer," he said. "Oh, man, this really hurts." Matt winced. "After this, you and me are buddies."

I said nothing in response, but I was already feeling vindicated. Bobby had been wrong about Matt, wrong about this scenario and the opportunity it offered. In the final analysis, Bobby had learned none of this night's lessons.

I was now standing more or less face-to-face with Matt Stefano. Only a few yards—and the woodpile—separated us.

"So what is it?" I asked him.

"You've got to come around here to see—and to get me loose."

I shrugged and walked toward the edge of the woodpile. I hadn't really expected to get him loose without walking back there, had I?

I rounded the edge of the woodpile, and stepped behind it with Matt. I looked down at the other boy's feet, saw his motorcycle boots and the tattered cuffs of his jeans.

"What's got hold of you, Matt? I don't see any—"

Matt's expression abruptly changed as he dropped his ruse. A sardonic grin spread across his face.

"Man, you are one dumbass sap, Schaeffer. I am so going to enjoy pounding the holy crap out of you."

I began to turn away, already making panicked calculations: How far back to the road? If I got a head start, could I outrun Matt?"

I never got the chance to find out. Before I could take any evasive action, Matt Stefano was upon me. He linked one booted foot behind one of my ankles and gave me a hard push. The night sky, a treetop, and the full moon spun across my vision as I went down. I hit the ground hard. I closed my eyes. A second later, I felt the impact—and the pain—reverberate throughout my body.

But that was only the prelude to the real pain. I felt a tremendous weight come down upon me. It felt like a small tree had fallen across my stomach. My eyes flew open, and Matt Stefano's face was only inches from mine.

Matt showed me his clenched fist.

"You've had this coming for a long time, Schaeffer."

A mixture of fear and shame prevented me from offering any response, let alone mounting a last-minute resistance. I had been brave tonight, yes; I had done great things, sure. And none of that had made me impervious to the attack of the same older bully who had long been the bane of my existence. The night might have transformed me—but it hadn't transformed me quite enough. To make matters worse, I had willingly walked into this obvious trap. I had placed myself on this ground.

Matt pulled his fist back, and I cringed in abject terror and resignation, waiting for the blow.

But the blow never came.

I heard Matt cry out in sudden surprise. At the same time, his weight shifted. A second later he was no longer completely on top of me. His weight shifted abruptly to one side.

A third person was among us: Bobby. Matt called out an expletive, and then Bobby hit him—hard.

I took advantage of the moment to work myself free of Matt's legs. Using both my arms and legs, I pushed myself away from him.

The fight that had only seconds ago been a one-sided match between Matt Stefano and me was now a contest between Matt Stefano and Bobby. Matt would probably have been able to throw a decent punch had he been standing; but kneeling on the ground as he was, Matt could manage no more than a wild, random swing in Bobby's direction.

Bobby, on the other hand, was standing erect, and was well positioned to make the most of his superior angle and balance. His next blow struck Matt squarely in the jaw. There was a sharp, sickening cracking sound—perhaps of one or several of Matt's teeth breaking.

"Ooomph!"

Matt toppled over. This might have been the end of the fight— except it wasn't. Bobby pounced on Matt during the latter's moment of pain-induced daze and weakness. Ironically, this was exactly what Matt had done to me not a minute ago.

"*Nagel—no!*" Matt cried out, just as a fist descended on his nose, smearing Matt's face and Bobby's fist with blood. This was followed by another blow to the face, and another.

And another. And another.

Bobby was sitting astride Matt's body, pummeling his face methodically, but with a rage that scared even me—and Bobby had come to *my* rescue. Bobby wasn't pulling his punches at all, he wasn't waiting for Matt to cry uncle or beg for mercy. The blows assumed a rhythmic quality, though each one struck with a crack or a dull, wet thud.

He's going to kill him, I thought. *Bobby is going to kill Matt Stefano.*

I would be lying if I said that there wasn't a part of me that relished the possibility. Matt had hectored and bullied me for a long time, and when I had extended an olive branch, he had betrayed my trust with deceit and violence.

But what Bobby was doing now went far beyond an act of adolescent retribution. This was—or would be—murder.

"Bobby!" I said. "Bobby, that's enough. He's down."

Bobby didn't stop, though—not until I walked over to the two of them, so close that I had to pull back as Bobby readied his next blow, lest I be struck by mistake.

"Come on, Bobby: that's enough."

I reached out and grabbed his hand. He looked back at me, fury in his eyes. For a second, I wondered if he might turn that bottomless, white-hot fury on me.

But instead he snapped out of it. He was breathing hard; and Matt Stefano, barely conscious, was no threat to either of us.

"All right," Bobby said, exhaling. "All right."

Bobby stood up from Matt Stefano's inert body. The latter looked at us through swollen eyes. Matt looked at Bobby, and then at me. I could not discern if there was any gratitude in Matt's gaze. A few minutes ago I had walked behind the woodpile with the intention of saving his life, fooled by ruse. Just now I had saved his life for real.

Bobby appeared ready to give Matt a parting kick in the ribs. Instead he just nudged him with his shoe. Matt lay still, obviously in no mood to provoke Bobby any further.

"Let's go," I said. "Leah's waiting for us at the road."

"Leah's waiting for *you*."

I started to protest, but Bobby waved me to silence. I did not argue. I saw that the front of his white shirt—worn to resemble a pirate's tunic—was stained with Matt Stefano's blood.

We trudged through the yard, toward the road, in silence.

"What happened back there?" Leah asked. Apparently she had seen little of the melee. She gasped when she saw Bobby's blood-stained shirt.

"Are you okay, Bobby?" she asked.

"I'm fine," Bobby replied sullenly. His tone made clear that he was in no mood for talking. We resumed our walk through the final length of our journey: Bobby once again pulled ahead of us, and Leah and I walked side-by-side.

I was watching Bobby's back, wondering what he might be thinking, when I felt Leah take my hand.

And then I felt less concerned about Bobby. Leah squeezed my hand and we continued along like that. I was surprised—and a little ashamed—at how good and complete and triumphant I felt then, despite all of the horrible things that had just happened.

WE ARRIVED BACK at our starting point without further problems. If there were any more evil things watching us, they stayed hidden. Bobby and I walked Leah to her house. Bobby waited at the road while I accompanied Leah up to her front door. Leah let herself in with her key. I waited on the front porch while Leah stepped inside. I listened to her exchange greetings with her parents. We were late, it seemed, by about a half an hour, and Mr. and Mrs. Carter expressed some surprise. Leah uttered a clumsy, half-baked excuse: The time had simply gotten away from us.

Leah stepped back out on the porch and closed the door behind her.

"It's normal," she said. "Everything. I—I think it's over."

"Is it ever really over?" I asked, not quite sure where that question had come from.

She gave me a curious look, then another smile that I became lost in.

"I'd like to kiss you one last time," I said, pressing my luck.

"Then do it, but be quick about it, before my father steps out here."

I leaned forward and kissed Leah, full and hard on the lips. I felt her arms wrap around me.

My God, was this—?

Yes, I told myself. This was. It was happening for me. Really.

"I'll talk to you tomorrow," she said, gently pushing away from me and breaking the kiss.

"Tomorrow."

Bobby was still waiting for me, surprisingly patient, when I returned to the road. He said nothing as we resumed the walk to my house.

"I'll get my dad to drive you home, of course," I said, when we reached my driveway.

Bobby slowly shook his head. "Look at me, Schaeffer. I'm a mess." He gestured to his bloodstained shirt.

"So what? My dad has seen blood before. He was in the army, you know."

"Yeah, but this is different."

"It's no big d—"

"Anyway, Schaeffer: Everything seems to be okay now. And to tell you the truth, I could kind of use a little walk by myself. To clear my head."

"Are you sure?" I didn't want to let Bobby walk the mile, more or less, between the edge of Shayton Estates and his house on Shayton Road. At the same time, I was oddly anxious to be away from him, at least for a while. He had helped me back there—there was no denying that. But in helping me, he had revealed a part of himself that was dark and perpetually angry, and possibly dangerous, even for me.

"I'm sure," Bobby said. I stood at the place where the driveway of my parents' house met the road, and watched him turn away, and begin his solitary walk home.

"Bobby!" I called out when he was a good distance away.

"Yeah?"

"Thank you—for what you did back there."

"Yep," Bobby said. He had barely paused.

WHEN I WALKED INSIDE, my younger sister Carrie was seated at the kitchen table. She was still wearing her Tinker Bell costume, though no depiction of Tinker Bell was probably ever quite so glum.

"Your father called," my mother said, appearing out of the adjacent living room. "He said he just couldn't break away—closing and all. He was hoping that you could take Carrie out after all, but trick-or-treat is over now." She glanced pointedly at the picture clock above the refrigerator—a pastoral scene with a crowing rooster and a red barn in the background. "In fact, trick-or-treat was over going on an hour ago."

My father arrived home barely ten minutes after I did, still clad in his suit and tie, even though it was now late in the evening. He didn't have to ask if I had come through for my sister. He had spoken to my mother earlier, who had reported me gone, and now Carrie's expression would have revealed whatever pieces of the puzzle were missing: Her almost-a-high-school-student big brother had gone out trick-or-treating, and left her behind.

My father didn't issue any loud rebukes or recriminations. A member of the Silent Generation, that wasn't his style. He merely looked at me and shook his head; and I felt all the more ridiculous: I had just kissed a girl seriously—romantically—for the first time, but I was dressed up like a pirate.

I went up to my room shortly thereafter. I was too wired to sleep, my emotions a mixture of exhilaration (over Leah, of course) and horror (over everything else). And beneath all that, there was a quiet and undefined sadness about Bobby: I had the feeling that tonight had marked a turning point in our relationship; and henceforth, things between us would never be quite the same.

I was mistaken, however, in my complacent belief that the curse was over. The ghost boy had said twelve hours, and twelve hours it was to be.

I drifted off to sleep early, but awoke sometime after 1 a.m. to find my room filled with horrific sights and sounds. There were shadows of great winged things moving across my walls in the moonlight. In the mirror above my dresser, a series of terrifying scenes materialized: It was like a kaleidoscopic view of Pieter Bruegel's famous painting, "The Triumph of Death". Skeletons were murdering the living— with blunt instruments, with axes and even saws; spectral executioners were creating fresh heaps of bodies. They were an army of grim reapers, waging a war against those of us who had the audacity to live and embrace the pleasures of the world.

But even as I glimpsed these things, I sensed that the curse was waning. These were images that could disturb me; they could probably not harm me. I closed my eyes tightly, and did my best to ignore the sounds of flapping wings and moaning victims. *Twelve hours*, I told myself. The night could only last so long. In the morning, it would be over.

21

It wasn't over, though, not really. Yes, the curse ended. But there was an aftermath. There is always an aftermath.

The following Monday, Matt Stefano showed up to school with his face badly bruised—leading to an immediate proliferation of rumors.

It was quite obvious to everyone that Matt Stefano had been on the losing end of a fight. The question was: Who had beaten him up?

As is often the case with the adolescent rumor mill, the story that the crowd embraced was somewhere between fiction and fact. Somehow it became known that Matt had mixed it up with Bobby and me—or maybe only Bobby, or maybe only me. For all I know, Bobby may have started the latter rumor.

In any event, I acquired an unearned reputation as a tough guy, even though the full truth of the matter was never conclusively established. Bobby was deliberately close-lipped about the details, dismissing all askers with a peremptory vagueness: He did not want to talk about it. Matt Stefano, needless to say, did not want to talk about it, either. Whichever version of the story was to be believed, Matt had tangled with seventh-graders and come out on the losing end.

Nor did Matt seek any retribution beyond that night. I made efforts to avoid him, of course; but some contact was inevitable in the microcosm of St. Patrick's. When we came face-to-face in the hallway or the boy's restroom, Matt ignored me as if I weren't there. There was to be no reconciliation, as I had quixotically allowed myself to hope for a few minutes that night, just before Matt's deception came to light. But nor, it soon became clear, was there to be further bullying. I regarded this as an acceptable compromise outcome. The following spring, Matt Stefano left St. Patrick's for Youngman High School. I thankfully declared myself done with him forever. I would see him again, as it turned out—though not for many, many years.

Leah, Bobby, and I never discussed the events of Halloween night. Just like before, neither of them wanted to talk about things that could not possibly have happened.

That wasn't the only change between the three of us. Leah and I gradually, somewhat awkwardly, evolved into something of an "item". She waited for me in the schoolyard after lunch and we talked—not hand in hand, but standing or sitting close together. I called her on the phone almost every night, even though I saw her at school and she lived just one street over. If I neglected to call (and sometimes I did, just so I wouldn't appear too besotted with her) she would call me.

We started going on "dates", too—in the makeshift ways that are necessary before driving licenses and access to cars. One of our parents (usually my father) would drive us to the cinema at Eastgate Mall. Over the next two years, while still in junior high school, we saw *Raiders of the Lost Ark*, *Chariots of Fire*, *E.T., the Extra-Terrestrial*, and *Rocky III*.

These were all safe movies that had no connection to the events of that night (which Leah and I had still not discussed in depth). When the horror movie *Poltergeist* was released in the summer of 1982 —the summer before we started high school—I didn't even suggest that we see it. I knew by that time that for Leah, such subject matter was—and always would be—strictly off-limits. I was on my own regarding any contemplation or search for answers concerning the events of Halloween night of 1980. Whatever else Leah brought to my life, she either could not or would not help me there. If I wanted to be with her, I sensed, then I had to maintain the careful and unspoken fiction that had solidified around the ghost boy, the head collector, Elmira, and George: Those things had simply not happened.

Bobby drifted away from Leah and me. I can't pinpoint the exact day when we ceased to be a threesome; but the schism began almost immediately after Halloween. Bobby had too much dignity to play the third wheel. The truth, moreover, was that the changed character of the relationship between Leah and me had made us need him less.

When I think back to what eventually happened to him, sometimes I wish we had needed him more. But we were young, mutually infatuated, and self-absorbed. We both still nodded to him in the halls at St. Patrick's; and once in a while he would join us for a walk home (though most of the time, he didn't). Then the eighth grade ended, and Bobby, too, disappeared into Youngman while Leah and I went on to Bishop Stallings.

While the lives of Bobby, Leah, and I were profoundly changed by the events of that night, we hadn't been the first ones to experience the curse. There was Jimmy Wilson, who lost his car that night, but escaped with his life. And then there was George—who lost his life while distracting the head collector so we could escape.

I don't know how Jimmy Wilson handled the destruction of his car—with the insurance company, police, etc. I don't know if he even reported the incident to the police. (What would he have told them, after all?) But I do know that the destruction was real; a few weeks later I saw Jimmy Wilson driving through the neighborhood in a used Ford Granada that was five or six years old. The Granada was a step down from the Nova, both in quality and prestige. But I imagine that Jimmy Wilson was grateful to have escaped with his life, if not his beloved hot rod.

After that night, Jimmy Wilson did his best to avoid us; and circumstances mostly allowed him to do that. He was seven years older than us, and he moved in different circles.

Sometimes he would drive past as Leah and I were walking. On these occasions, Jimmy always became suddenly distracted by something in the distance, or began fiddling with the radio of his Granada. He would not acknowledge us; he would not look us in the eye after what he had done.

Jimmy Wilson is now well into his fifties, and a senior executive for a major corporation in Cincinnati. He now goes by the name James Wilson instead of Jimmy. Not long ago, I saw a brief write-up about him in the *Cincinnati Business Weekly,* which included a studio portrait of him in a business suit. The curly hair of his teenage years had been replaced by the balding, closely cropped pate of a middle-aged executive. His jowls had gone slack and he had gained some weight. I still recognized him, though, as the long-ago young man who had deserted us on that night in 1980.

I wondered: *Does he still think about it? Is James Wilson still haunted in his dreams by Ronald, Larry, and Jerry? Do they still pay him the occasional Halloween night visit?*

George, on the other hand, would never resurface. His death by the blade of the head collector had been all too real. But the rest of the world would never know the truth.

No missing person report was filed for the better part of a week. George lived alone, he was retired; and his absence wasn't noted until mail and newspapers began to accumulate, and a concerned neighbor walked over to find George gone, and his back door left ajar.

Then it was reported that George Chambers, resident of 678 Meadowridge Drive, was missing. No evidence of foul play (other than the open door) was discovered. George's headless body, and the blood from his dismemberment, had been "taken care of" by then— perhaps by the forces that conspired to keep the details of the Halloween curse a secret from all but the unlucky few.

Neither Leah nor I said anything about our encounter with the old man—and neither did Bobby, so far as I know. There was a police investigation, and the disappearance of George Chambers, aged 64, became a minor obsession around the neighborhood for a while. The police investigation was given extensive coverage in the county papers, and in the *Cincinnati Post* and the *Cincinnati Enquirer.*

George's closest living relatives, a sister and a nephew from out of town, occasionally visited the house and arranged for the maintenance. George's house stood empty for the better part of two years while the police looked for George's killer, or maybe his body in one of the area's many wooded gullies and bramble-choked meadows.

But in the end there was nothing for the police to find, no definitive conclusion for them to reach. George Chambers had simply disappeared; and with no surviving spouse or children, there was no one to lead the effort to keep the investigation active, to keep hope alive. In early 1983 George Chambers was declared legally dead. The house on Meadowridge Drive was sold, and these proceeds—along with whatever other assets George had owned—were disposed of according to his will. I would imagine that the out-of-town nephew and his mother received something.

Many, many years later, as the twentieth century became the twenty-first, there was another break in the George Chambers case, though no one recognized it as such, so far as I know. A construction crew was clearing a hillside for a new housing development off Clough Pike, when a headless skeleton turned up in the shovel of a backhoe. The hillside was about two miles from George's house, which had since changed owners several times.

This gruesome discovery caused a real buzz, of course. Forensic investigators determined that the skeleton had been in the ground for many years—perhaps a hundred or more. That might have been true; but I believe that was George's skeleton that turned up in the shovel bucket of that backhoe, and the analyzed age of his bones was somehow altered by what had happened. What were the chances of another headless body being buried around here a hundred years ago?

But then again, how long had random people been encountering these spirits on certain Halloween nights? So I suppose that the forensic experts might have been right, after all. In any event, by the time the headless skeleton was discovered in the spring of 2000, the mysterious case of George Chambers had been long since forgotten, and there was no official effort to establish a connection.

As I've said, my father was disappointed in my decision to go out trick-or-treating that night. I had left Carrie behind, and she moped around the house for the rest of that week.

My father's disappointment eventually faded, though. I had been self-absorbed and self-centered, sure. But what adolescent isn't self-absorbed and self-centered from time-to-time? Like so many trivial incidents between parents and children, it was simply forgotten over time, absorbed into the larger flow of our relationship. By the time Halloween of 1981 rolled around, there was no question in anyone's mind that I was too old for the ritual of trick-or-treating. Everything had changed: Leah and I were a couple by then, and Bobby had grown distant. Moreover, I would not have risked a repeat of the previous Halloween for all the candy in Ohio. That particular childhood ritual was permanently tainted for me.

My father died in 2009 of pancreatic cancer—the malignant and fast-moving kind. He was diagnosed in early March, and by November he was gone. I was 41 then and he was 71.

Dad was, I recall thinking, too young to pass; and I was too young to lose my father. But he had lived long enough to know his four grandchildren, and he died surrounded by family and friends. These realizations did not stop me from privately shedding tears in the days immediately following his death. They have, however, brought me solace in the years since then.

Carrie has also long since forgotten about the Halloween on which I left her forlorn at our kitchen table. Carrie is in her early forties and married; her two children are in high school.

I wish I could report to you a happy ending for Bobby as well. After he drifted away from Leah and me, Bobby began a descent of sorts, that I observed, but made no real effort to halt or correct. I told myself that there was nothing I could have done, though I now know the truth: I might have said something to Bobby, I might even have partially befriended him again, had I not been so thoroughly absorbed in my own life—which followed a more or less positive trajectory after that Halloween night.

After Leah and I went to Bishop Stallings and Bobby went to

Youngman, our contact with him all but ceased. One night in the summer before our senior year, Leah and I ran into him in the parking lot of a local restaurant. We had been having dinner; Bobby had been drinking with his new friends at the edge of the parking lot.

Bobby greeted us, but there was something about his manner that was reserved, distant, and vaguely threatening. Not to mention his blatant intoxication. Leah and I extricated ourselves from the encounter as quickly as we could; and as I was starting up the car, Leah said from the seat next to me: "What do you think will happen to him, I mean long term?"

I remember answering Leah's question with a shrug. I had no answers for her. Anyway, that was Bobby's problem, wasn't it? I certainly didn't want to see him sink, but if he was going to swim—it would be up to him.

All long-term questions about Bobby Nagel were cut short two summers later, when Bobby, then aged twenty, died in an automobile accident with two other people. It was a horrible accident—made bad by more than simply the youth and numbers involved. Bobby had been driving, and the subsequent autopsy revealed that his blood alcohol level was twice the legal limit in Ohio at that time.

One of the other passengers was Molly Evans—the girl with whom Bobby had reached "second base" in our seventh grade year. On the night of her death, Molly Evans had been Bobby's girlfriend of two years. She had also been five months pregnant. Bobby had gotten a lot farther than second base with Molly. What he hadn't done was manage to drive with seven or eight drinks in his system— the estimated amount of beer, shots, and wine coolers that he'd consumed before driving his car off a winding two-lane country road and into the trunk of a massive hickory tree.

If this were a made-up story, Matt Stefano would have died young as well. Not that I'd ever wish anyone dead, mind you, but wouldn't there have been some cosmic justice in that?

Matt, however, lived for many years after Bobby Nagel was dead— and (it pains me to admit it) mostly forgotten. As far as I know, Matt

Stefano is alive today, even as I write these words. I see no reason why he should not be.

I ran into Matt less than a year ago, last spring. I was working on a home improvement project: an extension of our deck. I went to the closest retail lumber store: an 84 Lumber located on Ohio Pike.

I went inside the store knowing exactly what I needed. I had done building projects before. (A few years ago I built a tool shed that's holding up quite nicely, in fact.) I went to the front desk and placed an order for some 2x4s and some 2x8s.

"No problem," the young guy at the front desk said, checking the store's inventory on a computer terminal. "We have plenty of both in stock. Just drive around back and ask for Matt; he'll take care of you."

I didn't think anything of the name Matt, of course. In the intervening years, I had known many Matts and Matthews. It's a common enough name, after all. I handed over my credit card for processing, without the slightest thought of Matt Stefano.

I drove my SUV back through the open gate of the fenced-in area where the store kept most of its lumber inventory. I spotted another store employee—a kid who might have still been in high school.

"The cashier told me to see Matt," I said, from behind the steering wheel. I held up my receipt.

"Oh, yeah," the kid said. "Matt's back there." He cocked a thumb toward a man sitting in a small, open cubicle, just inside the warehouse area. "You want me to get him for you?"

"No thanks." It was one of the first truly summerlike days of the year, and I didn't mind stepping out of the SUV. Besides, I might get to handpick my pieces. I'm particular about my lumber.

The kid shrugged as if to say, 'whatever'. "Matt's back there," he repeated, cocking the thumb again.

I put my SUV in park and turned off the ignition. It was, as I've said, a glorious springtime afternoon, and the warm, fragrant air was invigorating. The glare of the midday sun on my face made me feel younger—in a good way. Thoughts of Halloween 1980 were a million miles away.

As I walked back into the warehouse area, the man at the desk either ignored or was unaware of my presence. He was older, perhaps a few years older than me. His height was difficult to gauge: He seemed to have a long body, but he was also stoop-shouldered. His hair was black with strands of gray. He was one of those middle-aged men who insists on wearing his hair long, years after such a hairstyle has ceased to fit him. The man's tangled, stringy locks obscured most of his face as he bent over his desk, writing on what appeared to be an invoice or bill of lading.

My footsteps echoed on the concrete floor of the warehouse. He was going to wait as long as possible to acknowledge me, then

"Excuse me," I said, my receipt from the cashier at the ready. "I have an order to pick up. They said Matt would help me. Are you Matt?"

"Sure am," he said, in a tone that was not exactly rude, but not overly polite, either. He finished his writing before he looked up at me.

More than three decades had passed since Matt Stefano had held me against the brick wall of St. Patrick's, threatening me with bodily harm. A lifetime stretched out between that afternoon at the lumber store, and the distant night when Matt Stefano tackled me behind the woodpile.

There are incidents and meetings, however, that can compress time, and make long spans of years disappear in a heartbeat. Despite the slack jowls, prematurely wrinkled face, and graying hair, I recognized Matt Stefano almost immediately. Then I noticed the nameplate on his desk: 'M. Stefano'.

There was no indication that Matt Stefano recognized me. He rolled his chair back from the desk, stood, and extended an open palm. He was as tall as I remembered him being, but he was different now: His body, like his face, was sagging. Here was a man who had either abused himself for decades or been sick. Possibly both.

"Let's see your receipt."

"Matt Stefano," I said, handing over my receipt.

"That's what the nameplate says," he repeated matter-of-factly. He still didn't get it. He didn't recognize me.

Then he read my receipt. My name was printed at the bottom along with my signature for the credit card payment. Matt Stefano looked up at me, suddenly understanding.

"I remember you," he said. "Jeff Schaeffer."

"I remember you, too."

"Kids. Crazy stuff back then, huh?"

He was trying to blow it off. He was trying to pretend like none of it ever happened. Like he had never held me against the wall, fearful and angry but powerless to do anything about it. Like he had not betrayed me that night—when I would have been perfectly willing to make peace with him.

He must have sensed at least some of my thoughts.

"Listen, Schaeffer. In case you're still mad about all that: If you'll recall, your friend gave me a pretty hard pounding. Beat the crap out of me, in fact. And everyone thought you did it. Yeah, I knew about that. You got credit for what Bobby Nagel did."

I said nothing.

"And I suppose you're wondering why I never tried to take revenge on you, never tried to catch you alone. I guess you could say that I was just ready to move on. Picking on you was suddenly more trouble than it was worth—if I had to mess with your friend Bobby as part of the bargain."

"Don't say his name," I said, suddenly a twelve-year-old boy in a middle-aged man's body. "You're not worthy of saying his name."

Matt Stefano snorted. "Okay. Fine. I know what happened to him. Of course that was a long time ago now, too, wasn't it? Damn shame. Bobby Nagel obviously wasn't my favorite person in the world, but I didn't want to see him go like—"

"Just stop."

"All right, I'll stop." He laid my receipt down on his desk. "So what do you want to do here, Schaeffer? Do you want me to get your lumber for you? Or do you finally want to fight me, after all these years? Is that what this is about?"

Before I could answer, Matt unbuttoned the first two buttons of his uniform shirt. With two fingers of his right hand, he traced over a white network of surgical scars.

"Pacemaker," he explained. "I got it put in two years ago. Almost killed me. I had to quit smoking, too. That almost killed me, too. Doctor told me I have emphysema. I sleep with an oxygen tank. Otherwise, when I sleep my blood oxygen content gets too low."

I shrugged. Did he want me to feel sorry for him? Did his misfortunes as an adult change what he had done as a child? At least he was still alive. Bobby had been dead for more than twenty-five years.

Or was I the one who was at fault here? I had had my chance to face Matt Stefano thirty-some years ago, and I hadn't been up to the task. Suppose I was to take my revenge on a much-diminished version of him? Would that be cheating?

And what was I thinking, anyway? I was a married man with two children who were almost adults. I was a responsible adult now. All of that business with Matt Stefano *had* been a long time ago, hadn't it?

Matt Stefano, moreover, hadn't killed Bobby Nagel—any more than I had tried to save him.

"Just get me my lumber please," I finally said.

Matt Stefano nodded, and we both tried to pretend that nothing had happened. He instructed me to back my SUV into the warehouse area. I walked back to my vehicle and did as he asked. We completed the rest of the transaction without exchanging more than half a dozen words.

And now I'll answer the final question of my narrative (among the questions that I *can* answer, anyway): I suppose you're wondering if Leah and I got married.

If this were a made-up story, that would be the perfect ending, wouldn't it? Leah and I would have been forever bound together as a result of what we'd shared that night.

Things didn't work out that way—not exactly.

We did date for a number of years—all through junior high and high school.

Leah and I were inseparable. Our relationship—which was fairly adolescent and innocent in junior high—became adult soon enough. It was Leah who introduced me to the wonders of sex, after much pleading and cajoling on my part, the night of our junior homecoming at Bishop Stallings. And if you want to get technical about it, I suppose you could say that I was the one who introduced her to those wonders, as well.

We briefly broke up during the spring of our junior year. Somehow a petty disagreement had resulted in a mutual conclusion that we should "see other people". That only lasted for a month. We weren't ready to see other people—at least not yet. When we graduated from Bishop Stallings High School in June 1986, Leah and I were voted runner-up for our class's "cutest couple". It still looked like a storybook ending for us.

But once in college, we drifted apart. Leah won a scholarship to the University of Notre Dame, which is located in the northernmost end of Indiana. I would have gone with her, but there was no way I could have won a scholarship to Notre Dame. Nor could I have afforded the tuition. For that matter, I would have been lucky to have even gained admission. Notre Dame was—and is—a fairly exclusive university.

So I attended the University of Cincinnati; and Leah and I settled into a long-distance relationship, separated by a four-hour drive, more or less. I told myself (and we told each other) that it would work. But I think I knew better, even then.

In those days before cell phones, text messages, or email, some effort was required for two college students to maintain regular contact across a long distance. At first we made the effort. We wrote each other letters (yes, snail mail) every week. I regularly called her at Notre Dame, and she called me. Leah shared an apartment (and a single phone line) with three other girls. Long-distance rates between Cincinnati and northern Indiana weren't cheap. We could talk, but only for limited periods of time.

Needless to say, this wasn't the same as being together in the same city, in the same neighborhood, attending the same school. I slowly began to realize that while Leah and I had legitimately had something, much of that something had been based on familiarity, proximity, and inertia. Our relationship wasn't the sort of epic love that could survive long periods of time apart; and it wasn't like we had a marriage and two kids to keep us together. We saw each other during the holiday break of that first year of college. Leah was still my girlfriend, but there was something pro forma about her affection. Something was up, I thought—but I didn't want to sound like the insecure jealous boyfriend. Things would work out, I told myself.

Or maybe they wouldn't. Gradually, our phone calls and letters became more perfunctory, and then they became more infrequent. Sometime in late February of that first year apart, I noticed a new trend: I would call Leah's apartment, and one of her roommates would tell me that she was "out". Questions regarding the hour of her return were met with vague evasions. Would I like to leave a message?

I wasn't completely surprised when Leah's "Dear John" letter arrived in the mail a few weeks later. I have long since lost her letter, and I don't remember her exact words, but it was a familiar story: Leah was a pretty young woman, and we had spent most of the past year apart. She had met someone else. She was in love with him.

Leah, to her credit, didn't refuse to talk to me again, or even go out of her way to avoid me. She called me, in fact, the day after the letter arrived. She offered to meet if I wanted to, to talk things out in person.

I replied that if she was in love with someone else, then there really wasn't much to talk about. I thanked her for her consideration, but no, I didn't see any point in meeting to talk about what was already a fait accompli, as far as Leah was concerned. She seemed relieved.

I moped for a while, as a young man is apt to do when his heart is truly broken for the first time. I considered calling her many times, and each time I restrained myself. It was over, I resolved, and nothing was to be gained by pleading. I should maintain my dignity.

That was a gloomy spring and summer for me. Leah was home for a few weeks; and she waved to me from a distance several times.

Most of that summer, I was later told, she spent in Colorado, where her new boyfriend was from.

The following September I was in the main library at the University of Cincinnati when I happened to notice an attractive, bespectacled girl reshelving books in the library stacks. On a whim and a prayer I said hello to her, then struck up a conversation. Thirty minutes later I had her phone number.

That was Eileen, my wife of more than twenty years. Like Leah, she's a lot smarter than I am—a wise man gravitates toward wiser women, I've always believed—and she's passed on her smarts to our daughters. Not to mention her good looks. Hannah and Lisa both favor their mother, with just enough traces of me.

I had no further contact with Leah for years—decades, in fact. She didn't show up at our class's tenth, fifteenth, or twenty-year reunions. By that time, my broken heart had long since healed, and I was very satisfied with how things had turned out, and my overall lot in life. I would have liked to have introduced Leah to Eileen, and maybe even met the man who had stolen Leah away from me so many years ago. (I had heard through the grapevine that Leah lived in Colorado, married to a man she'd met while a student at Notre Dame.) Leah, however, remained completely absent from my life for all those years.

Then in 2011 I finally got around to setting up an account on Facebook. I proceeded to reestablish online contact with all of my old Bishop Stallings High School classmates; I had lost track of most of them over the years, except for brief conversations at reunions.

One day I received a "friend" request from Leah Carter Barrett. I immediately accepted it, of course; and I allowed myself, after so long, a look at Leah's new life. She and her husband ran a small business out in Colorado. They had two teenage children: a son and a daughter.

Leah and I chatted back and forth for a while using Facebook's messaging system. There was no direct mention of our former relationship, of course—only talk about our current lives. The real estate brokerage that Leah and her husband owned in Colorado had been hit by the real estate downturn of 2008, but business was improving. Her son wanted to go to Notre Dame just like his parents had. Her daughter was thinking about medical school. Et cetera.

These online conversations eventually tapered off, just like our conversations had tapered off during the 1986-7 school year, when she was at Notre Dame and I was in Cincinnati. We could only exchange so much bland personal data without really talking. And really talking—the way we used to in high school—was probably impossible for us now. We were no longer the two teenagers who had briefly fallen in love. Leah was another man's wife. And I was happily married to Eileen.

One evening about a year ago, I sent Leah a Facebook message. This was after we had all but stopped messaging each other with any regularity.

I wrote, *"Leah: Do you ever think about it? I'm just curious."*

The next morning, I found her reply in my inbox. *"Think about what?"* she'd typed. She included one of those smiley face emoticons with her message, probably so it wouldn't seem too abrupt.

What, indeed, I thought. I considered my cryptic message from Leah's perspective. I might have been asking if she ever thought about 'us', or maybe Bobby's death at nineteen. Or maybe the events of that Halloween night—which Leah had refused to talk about even then. Why had I dared to hope that she might be willing to discuss those events now, after so many years had passed?

I typed: *"I mean: Do you ever think about how much time has passed? About how old we're getting?"*

Her response came less than an hour later: *"All the time! Every cold winter morning when I get out of bed, especially! I hope you and your family are doing well, Jeff. Take care. Leah."*

EPILOGUE

We *are* doing well, in the big scheme of things—despite the death of my father (and Eileen's mother, just last year).

I have no cause to complain, really: At the age of forty-six, I have achieved a reasonable level of affluence and career success. I'm still married to the same woman. And I adore my daughters.

I still have my health. I can still manage the occasional morning jog and my twice-weekly trips to the gym. I've dodged all of the big bullets so far: heart disease, cancer, etc.

That said, I can feel that fire of youth, which once pushed me so relentlessly, starting to fade. Sex isn't the driving, passionate force that it was at the age of eighteen or twenty-five.

But it's become something else with Eileen: Something calm, reliable, and a testament to our long lives together. That's not a bad way to grow old, all things considered.

I have lived long enough to marvel at how the world is changing. Since that long-ago election of 1980, we have had four more presidents. Ronald Reagan, the man who became president with that election, is now an object of nostalgia. The major issues of that time: the arms race with the Soviet Union, the Cold War, have become historical footnotes.

I sometimes tell my daughters about "the way things used to be," back when there was no Internet, and we used manual typewriters to type reports for school. Mostly they listen indulgently, but they occasionally roll their eyes—just like I did when my dad used to go on like that.

I want to tell them much more: how good friends and loved ones can be taken from you—sometimes by death, and sometimes simply by the way they change...by the ways in which *you* change.

As I drive home from Walmart with Lisa's birthday gift, I count my many blessings.

Yes, the Halloween of 2014 is almost here. Halloween comes inexorably every year; and this year I've seen the head collector already.

I'm not overly worried about him, though. Not that I have any illusions of immortality, mind you. Something will eventually take my life—but the head collector won't. I am no longer the twelve-year-old boy I once was. The head collector had his chance at me long ago, and he came out on the losing end of that confrontation. Momentarily brave and extraordinarily lucky, I managed to beat him.

With what I hope is the right balance of pride and humility, I remember those others who were not so brave—and those who were not so lucky.

MORE HORROR TITLES FROM EDWARD TRIMNELL

Additional horror fiction from Edward Trimnell available on Amazon:

Revolutionary Ghosts (New in 2019!)

The year is 1976, and the Headless Horseman rides again.

Eleven Miles of Night

A college student takes a walk down the most haunted road in Ohio in pursuit of a cash prize. Supernatural horror for fans of Stephen King!

Luk Thep

An American businesswoman travels to Thailand. Something evil follows her home.

Hay Moon and Other Stories: Sixteen Modern Tales of Terror and Suspense

Zombies, vampires, aliens, forest creatures, vengeful ghosts, and human villains. 16 monstrous tales for fans of Stephen King and Ray Bradbury.

Made in the USA
Middletown, DE
02 February 2020

84081941R00125